Hide & Seek

Hide & Seek is Clare Sambrook's first novel, and has already been translated into twelve languages. She lives in Cumbria, where she is working on her next book.

To the bears

Hide & Seek

Clare Sambrook

CANONGATE

Edinburgh · New York · Melbourne

First published in Great Britain in 2005 by
Canongate Books Ltd, 14 High Street,
Edinburgh EHI ITE

This edition published in 2006

3

British Library Cataloguing-in-Publication Data
A catalogue record for this book is available on
request from the British Library

I 84195 695 3 (10-digit ISBN)
978 I 84195 695 4 (13-digit ISBN)

Typeset by Palimpsest Book Production Limited,
Polmont, Stirlingshire
Printed and bound in Great Britain
by Clays Ltd, St Ives plc

www.canongate.net

End of term

I

The grown-ups held an inquiry into how a child came to disappear, but they didn't name names like they do when children let grown-ups down. They talked about a catalogue of errors as if mistakes were something that turned up in the post and got paid for later.

I had my own ideas. I blamed the driver, and, in different orders depending on how I was feeling:

Mr Pratt — really, that was his name — the larkiest teacher in our school, who was so free and easy he didn't bother to take a register on the bus.

My brother, Daniel Pickles, who was going on five, though the way he acted sometimes you'd never believe he was so old.

Dan's invisible friend, Biffo.

And me, Harry Pickles, that summer aged nine and a bit.

Now that enough time has gone by and I can talk about those days it feels right to begin, not with the coach trip and the day things went wrong, but the day before, when my Auntie Joan married Otis, which people kept saying was the start of something wonderful.

I think of my mum pounding down the stairs in her slinky silver dress.

'And what do you think you are doing?'

I was sitting on Daniel's face. It was obvious what I was doing. I pretended Mo wasn't there, let rip another one.

'Phwoagh,' said Daniel.

'Harry! That's disgusting!' When she was cross she got more Irish. 'Will you stop it. What's this about?'

Mo never thought to break us up before the interrogation. I counted eight lumps of cotton wool between her toes, admired the way her purple toenails gleamed and took my time about it while Dan puffed and wriggled between my legs. When I'd used up all my ammo I said,

'Dan's bugging me again.'

'Daniel, what have you to say for yourself?'

A muffled whine came out of him.

'Will I spank the pair of you?' She never did. I decided it was time to hop off.

'Harry won't help me find Bang Bang,' Daniel whined.

'We've no time to worry about Bang Bang today. Harry, I don't know why you feel obliged to torture your brother and Daniel I don't know why you put up with it.'

She had the answer right there if she thought about it.

'Will you look at your clothes!'

They were crumpled.

'We'll have those shirts off and ironed again.' She clucked us into the laundry room and we pulled off our horrible pink shirts.

'I want to be a fireman,' Daniel said.

I agreed with him on that. We had real fire-fighters' uniforms that whispered as you walked, with cool silver bands that shimmered in the dark and proper helmets, not plastic ones. We weren't allowed to wear them to the wedding. Oh, no. We had to wear poncy pink shirts to match the bridesmaids.

Barechested, we sat on the tumble-dryer. I tried not to kick my heels against it. Mo pressed under the buttons. Her nearly black eyebrows snuggled closer together. I could see right down her bazongers.

'Absolutely no more fighting today,' she said. 'You know exactly what's required of you.'

No way was I going to do that.

She said, 'We're all Joan's got.' She meant on account of Mo and Joan had no parents.

'You don't want to spoil Joan's big day, do you?'

We didn't. We really didn't. So we shook on it.

'Sorry, Harry.'

'Sorry, Daniel.'

Daniel smiled at me. I didn't smile back.

Mo put the iron down, said, 'I've one little favour to ask you,' and helped Daniel on with his shirt.

Dan shrieked. Then I smiled.

Mo whisked off the shirt and shook it cool. Typical Dan, didn't complain or anything. She helped him on with it again.

'Not everyone is aware, as you are, that Joan and Otis live together, and there is no need today of all days for any unexpected announcements from you. Understood?'

'Understood, Mo,' I said. It sounded like secrets. We weren't supposed to have those.

Dan fumbled with his buttons and said in that dreamy

5

way of his, 'I liked it when Joan lived here, when Otis got the girlfriend.'

Mo shot us both a how-did-you-know-that look. I didn't know that's why Joan had come to stay that time, couldn't believe it, that Otis would leave us for another woman.

Mo bit her lip, gently – she had her wedding face on.

'Today is the beginning of something wonderful for Joan and Otis. Let's forget about the past.'

I wouldn't go on about it but I wouldn't forget.

Dan jumped off the dryer – 'Da-Daaah!' – showed off his buttons.

Mo said, 'Good boy, yourself!' I don't know why. It wasn't rocket science.

Dan said, 'If we had a television we could plug it in and switch it on and –'

I mouthed, 'Not now, Daniel,' in perfect time as Mo said it out loud.

Me and Dan were fed, brushed, ironed, combed and fighting to stand on the tile where the sun shone when Pa swept into the kitchen, drop-dead handsome and smelling of lime. No pink on him.

He held out his arms to us. 'My beauties!'

My Auntie Joan used to say we had big brown come-to-bed-with-me eyes with extra long lashes like Pa's.

'Boys aren't beautiful, boys are smart,' Daniel said.

'You boys are beautiful and smart,' said Pa. 'And very nearly late. Come on. Of all people we have to be on time.'

The wedding was smack bang in the middle of Notting Hill, just like us. We only had to walk out of our house, across the garden square, around the corner and up the church steps. Forty-five seconds, it took, if you got a move on. I timed it.

'A tent!' Dan gasped the minute he got out of the house. You'd think the Martians had landed.

'It's a marquee, Daniel,' I said. 'For after the wedding,' in case he still didn't get it.

In next door's garden Shy Geoffrey popped his head out from behind *The Times* to tell us something. Something nice, most likely, Good Luck, or Have a Nice Wedding, something like that. You never could tell exactly on account of how he mumbled.

Out in the square Mrs Gomez was throwing a wobbly because someone, and They'd Better Not Think She Didn't Know Who They Were, had left the hosepipe running. She broke off to do a wolf-whistle for us.

'Nice dress, Mo,' said Sebastiano's mum as we strolled by. Then she turned and bellowed at the bushes, 'You'll have it cold or not at all!'

Leaves moved, but there was no sight of Sebastiano, who was a master of camouflage and allergic to houses.

We passed the den. Cal blew a salute on the conch shell. Pa waved.

Mo said, 'I see you've got it back then, Callum.'

Me, Cal and the other big boys had been playing Lord of the Flies til Milly's dad had his sense of humour failure and confiscated the shell. Milly was a pig we were hunting with spears. She was two. She didn't mind. She'd helped us gather firewood for the spit.

Seb's mum shouted, 'Callum, have you seen Sebastiano?'

Cal selected stones for his catapult, pretended not to hear. We had a code of honour, you see.

When we got to the corner Mo dropped her keys and bent down to pick them up. Pa gave her a whack on the behind. She slapped his arm.

'Will you stop that, Dominic!'

I could tell she liked it, though. Luckily Cal was taking aim at the one-eyed cat and didn't see.

I don't need to tell you much about the wedding. They're all the same, aren't they? Everyone whispered about whether Joan would turn up on time. She did, though. I wasn't nervous until the pastor asked if any of us knew a reason why Otis and Joan shouldn't get married. Pa knew some reasons. I hoped he wouldn't say them. The pastor left a huge long silence as if he knew one too. I held my breath for luck, closed my eyes and tried to figure out that row I'd heard Mo and Pa at in the bathroom.

'Not that again,' said Pa.

''Twas you brought it up.' Mo's voice strained.

'I only said.'

'I heard you.'

I didn't hear the next bit. Pa had the taps running. When he turned them off I caught,

'You know how intelligent women can be blinded by that sort of man.'

'What sort, exactly?'

He shook his shaving foam. 'Handsome. Charming. Stylish.' Then he squirted. 'And the boxing.'

8

'What about the boxing?'

'It's so . . . It's all blockheads and brutes, Mo.'

'Dom! What is your problem?'

'Let's leave it.'

'You're the one keeps bringing it up.'

I heard the scrape of Pa's razor, the killer one he got off his dad.

'All right, Mo.' He said it softly, like something danger-ous was coming. 'Ever seen him reading a book?'

Nothing from Mo. Must be tick-ticking towards one of her explosions.

'Oh and we're such a cultured pair.' Her voice had laugh-ter in it, actually. 'Mo Tully, Me and My Boys.'

'Your column's very good, hun.' He was stretching his face, shaving round his mouth, most likely.

'It's hardly Dostoyevsky, Dom. And as for you.'

'What about me? Bugger! Ouch!'

'I hardly think a lifetime's subscription to the *Lancet* counts as culture.'

'All I meant was –'

'Dom. Please don't let me think the father of my babies is a snob.'

Pa let out a sigh. 'Maybe I am. Yes. Probably it's me. You know how much I care about Joanie.'

'Honey,' she said, 'you're dripping blood on the floor.'

Plop! Plop! Big Plop! Only Mo could win an argument and poo all at once.

Daniel sneezed. Flowers did that to him. But it was all right. He used the handkerchief like Mo had told him.

Whatever Pa was thinking he didn't say it and the pastor got right on with the vows.

Joan, it turned out, was actually called Meredith Joan. That was news to some people. Not me and Dan. We'd found out in rehearsals.

I thought we were home and dry but then came 'To Have and To Hold,' and Otis, well, how can I tell you? Otis, who could skip non-stop for a whole entire hour, do thirty press-ups with Daniel clinging to his back, Otis cried. I mean really cried, sobbed out loud. I nearly died of embarrassment.

Daniel, like an idiot, stepped between Otis and Joan, grabbed Otis's thumb and gave it a squeeze. Otis stopped crying and ruffled Dan's hair. Then I wished I had thought of it.

After that everything went according to plan. No-one fainted. The ring wasn't lost. Me and Dan were brilliant pageboys. We didn't fight, fart or upset the bridesmaids.

I had a bit of trouble when Otis and Joan got to the stuff about honouring each other's bodies. My lips twitched. I felt the giggles coming on. But I was ready. I clenched my teeth and in my head I listed my all-time favourite Spurs team, including substitutes.

I expect you know about wedding receptions – chicken salad, Christmas cake and speeches that make your neck ache. It wasn't like that at Otis and Joan's wedding. The grown-ups had crawly things that would tap-dance off the plates if you didn't stick your fork in quick. I had my own special plantains mashed up by Otis's mum with her secret ingredient. And Dan had one jacket potato with Lurpak, his favourite meal in the world.

For pudding there was black chocolate mousse. Otis and Joan stood up, thanked everyone, said how much they loved each other, and – this bit made me puke – Otis thanked Daniel, for 'bringing us together in the first place.'

It was true, though.

I could just see Dan Dan, fat, stupid and two, trying to squeeze between the café railings in Holland Park. He got his head through all right, but his shoulders wouldn't pass and when he tried to back out he was stuck. He didn't cry, not straightaway. He grasped the railings either side and slid his head up and down, trying to find a bigger gap. There wasn't one. He moved his head round as far as it would go, lifted one foot off the ground. That didn't work, so he stopped and stood, thinking. I crept up behind him, gave him a shove. He yelped. Still he didn't cry.

I looked around for someone to help us. With a bit of luck I'd sort it and Mo would never know. Just the other side of the railings a pregnant woman and a toddler had a picnic on a rug. No use at all. Beyond them, some lanky boys played football. One snatched up the ball and jabbed his finger at the others. They seemed like tough boys to me. At the far end of the park, people played noiseless tennis. Daniel made a sort of gurgling sound.

I ran up the café steps to fetch Mo and Joan. They would have seen us if they hadn't been eating ice-cream and laughing. I told them what Daniel was doing, got the gurgling off perfect. They stopped laughing and dashed for the railings. I hung back to rescue their chocolate flakes. They'd dropped their cornets, you see.

When I caught up, Mo was saying, 'It's all right, Dan Dan, it's all right,' in a way that told him it was not all right at all. I wiped chocolate from my mouth. Dan's bottom lip quivered.

Joan said in a put-on cheery voice, 'This is a job for Dangermouse.'

The sky darkened. I saw leaves vibrate. Dan cried.

Joan said, 'Harry, fetch my bag please would you, darling?'

She probably carried important life saving equipment about on account of she was a nurse at the hospital. I raced for the bag, held it out while she fumbled in it and came up with a bottle. It said Body Shop on it and something about carrots. She smeared orangey stuff over Daniel's ears.

'Steeeeenks!' Daniel blubbed.

His neck grew fatter. Mo gripped him by the arms and wailed, 'Try to relax!'

Dan's face turned purple. Then the rain came. We didn't have anoraks.

That toddler screamed and kicked at picnic things its mother tried to gather up. Tennis players ran for cover. Footballers bickered and pulled on their anoraks. I licked chocolaty rain from my lips.

Joan said, 'Let's call the fire brigade.'

Fantastic! I'd never seen anyone do that in my life before.

Joan dived into her bag, came up with a mobile phone and dropped it, on account of the rain and the moisturiser. She picked it up, punched 999.

Rain dripped off my nose and I shivered. I needed a pee. It was ages before anyone answered.

Daniel was only whimpering by the time I saw a dot

moving towards us from way beyond the tennis courts. The dot turned into a fire-fighter — he had his helmet on and everything. He sprinted like a god or Linford Christie. Before it seemed possible he appeared, handsome and black, towering over us the other side of the railings. He'd brought a crowbar and a calm that worked instant magic on all of us.

I wanted him to notice me. He was looking at Daniel. He dropped to his haunches alongside my brother, put his face close and smiled. They might have been the only two people in the park.

'I'm very good at this,' he said and I believed him.

He pulled off the helmet, passed it to me. Heat came up out of it. He put the crowbar on the ground, took hold of one railing, got his heavy boot against the other. Dan's soft baby hair stroked the boot's muddy ridges. The fireman tensed, closed his eyes, breathed out through his nose. Mo raised a weak hand. The railings bent like Curly Wurlies. Daniel fell forward. Before his face could hit the ground the fireman caught him one-handed, passed him through the gap and into Mo's arms. It all happened in a moment and that moment I fell in love with Otis.

Auntie Joan took a lot longer about it.

Otis's family was bonkers. It spread like nits and I caught it. Me and Dan actually danced with the bridesmaids. Mine could speak Spanish, play violin and football. She said 'see y'around', when we'd finished. Otis's mum said I was an excellent dancer and it was nice for Otis to have boys in the family. He had two little brothers, but they were men, so didn't count. I told her I couldn't see Daniel turning

13

into a man and she laughed. I began to know how adults felt when they were tipsy.

We were the last children up at the party. Dan lay across some chairs under Otis's jacket, his arms flung out. I could easily drop a grape into his wide open mouth, watched the dancing instead. Couples stuck together swayed to mushy music. Coloured lights skittered the floor.

To keep myself from sleeping I tried counting fire-fighters. It would have been easier if they'd brought their axes or something.

I held a competition in my head for the best-looking couple. Mo and Pa had to be contenders. Pa's hand covered the small of Mo's back, pressed her close, seemed he was sniffing her hair. Joan had blue laughing eyes and shiny black hair just like Mo's, only Joan looked like she might float off the floor, up, up through the top of the tent, that's how happy she was. Luckily Otis had his strong arms around her. Really they should have won. I mean, it was their wedding. I gave it to Mo and Pa anyway, by a whisker.

Daniel startled like a baby. I put my hand on his chest, said, 'It's all right. You can stay sleeping,' and he did.

Next thing I knew Pa had me propped against our front door while he went through all his pockets for the keys. Mo had them. Pa carried me in and up the stairs. Behind us Mo knocked Daniel's head against the banister.

From inside his sleep Dan groaned, 'Everyone's got a television.'

Mo laughed, 'Not now, Daniel.'

Pa dumped me on my bed in the dark. He was trying

to be gentle. It wasn't working. He had difficulty with my shoes.

'Velcro,' I said, then he managed it.

He undid my trousers, pulled them off by the ends, unbuttoned my shirt, left it on. He was rough and I liked it. He didn't bother with my boxers or my socks.

'Teeth, Pa.'

'Not tonight, sweet boy.'

Pa pulled the duvet up to my chin, pressed it round me. He leaned down to kiss me, jabbed his nose in my eye. He kissed my forehead, stroked my hair, murmured something mushy. I couldn't make out the words. His breath smelled of wine. He had smoked a cigar. He felt bristly.

A tube train trundled by and then another one. They sounded tired, like they were heading home to bed.

D'dee D'dee, said the trains. *D'dee D'dee.*

I heard Mo tiptoe down the stairs from Dan's room. She met Pa on the landing. I heard low, teasing voices. They seemed to be wrestling. There was giggling and shushing. It must have been the last night I went to sleep feeling safe.

2

Barrr-bados, that's how Otis said it, Barrr-bados was a tiny green triangle floating in the sea.

'Are they there yet?'

Mo leaned over me, her face touching my hair. She thumbed through the atlas. The Indian Ocean flicked by, Pakistan and Tibet, Italy and France.

'They're here, love. Gatwick Airport.'

'Oh.' I stirred my Cheerios.

Pa dropped huge vitamin C tablets in two glasses of water, gave one to Mo, with a spoon.

'Take this, it'll make you better.'

She watched it fizz, it looked like blood in water, she stirred it quietly and sipped.

Pa shook coffee beans into the grinder. They made a soft sound as they landed.

I said, 'I hope the plane doesn't crash.'

'Harry, don't say such a thing. And not so loud.'

'I was only saying, Mo. I hope it doesn't.'

Pa pressed the button. Mo put her fingertips to her temples, closed her eyes. When she opened them again they were bloodshot. Pa tipped the coffee into the cafetiere, poured boiling water. Through the steam I saw the Picasso picture above the table, the really wild one, with monsters and jagged lights and people strewn about.

Dan bounced in wearing his Superman jimjams, pants over the top.

'You're full of fun,' Mo said.

'Bang Bang came back! She's back in her cage! Come and look, Mo! Look, Pa!'

Pa said, 'I'm so happy for you, darling,' and pushed the plunger.

'Dan Dan, that's great.' Mo's eyes flickered over me. I searched for Barbados.

'I said she'd come home,' Dan told the empty chair. 'Can we take Bang Bang to Legoland?' Brilliant idea. We'd lose her there for good.

'No, darling,' said Mo and Pa together.

Dan said, 'Are you coming, Mo?'

'Honey, I'd love to but I have to stay and do the column.' She'd best not put me and Daniel's hamster in it.

'Is everything at Legoland made of Lego?'

Daniel had been asking that all week and he was facing Biffo's way, so we didn't answer him. Pa poured Mo's coffee. Most of it actually made it into her cup.

In the school car park stood Mr Pratt wearing a white T-shirt and red shorts. He matched the colours of the coach. Had he planned it that way? He might have done. Mr Pratt would do anything for a laugh.

He said, 'What's up, Doc?' and shivered.

Pa shook his hand, did some cheery grown-up stuff, then gave a little salute to Piggy, waving madly from the back of the bus. Even hungover, bristly and standing next to the most popular teacher in our school, Pa looked like the kind of dad that everyone liked. He could have kissed me in front of the guys, but he kissed Daniel and patted me on the back.

'Look after each other,' he said as we climbed onto the bus.

Dan had to sit near the front because of his travel sickness. I sat with him. Behind us Parimal from Dan's class was crying already, the big baby – he'd sat on his crisps. Soon as we'd waved Pa off I scooted to the back where Peter and the boys had saved me a seat, in the middle of all places. Pete's little brother Stanley had nabbed a window seat.

'I spy with my little eye,' Peter was saying. 'Something beginning with D, something not on the bus.'

'A dog,' said Piggy.

'Drag racer,' said Terry, the new boy. We'd agreed to let him sit with us to give him a try-out for the gang, the gang being me and Peter, and Piggy sometimes.

'A dog,' Stan piped up.

'I said that!' said Piggy.

'I said it first!' said Stanley.

Peter shushed Stanley. Quite right too. Stanley was in Dan's class. He shouldn't have been sitting with us at all. I closed my eyes, tried not to let it bother me.

Pete was great, my best mate and everything, I'd known him all my life, but sometimes, you know, he could be a bit wet. He hated getting in trouble, never sweared or anything. And the way he treated Stanley. It wasn't right. Like he was equal. Even before the little ones joined our school, Peter wouldn't shut up about Stanley.

'He's dead fast, Harry.'

We were lying in gang HQ, the school sandpit. I had one ugly frog in my sights.

'Stan's got premier league potential,' Peter said.

I flicked a pebble off the back of my hand.

'Gotcha!' On the bum.

Stan would have to climb his way up the lower divisions like anyone else.

'Stanley's almost as fast as you are, Harry.' Not likely. I was probably the fastest boy runner in the world.

I took aim.

'He's really triffic at juggling.'

Flicked and missed.

Our Dan ran like a girl, threw like one too.

'Dan and Stan, it'll be brilliant,' said Peter.

'Terrific,' I said.

Fantastic Stan and Spastic Dan. I knew it would be a disaster.

But it wasn't, not in the way I'd expected. Stan was all right. Nothing special. But, Dan? Dan strolled around school like he'd been there forever, sticking his fat little fingers into everyone's business. And, you know what? They liked it. Dan, in his own twerpy way, was a star.

That first term some art students came and stuck Thomas the Tank Engine on the outside bog wall. They had pins in their faces, rolled their own cigarettes, smoked them by the urinals — that's where Piggy found the leftovers. We were told not to bother them and nobody did.

Except Dan. He'd pop over most days and chat with the lady in charge who wore tiny tight T-shirts over the biggest bazongers me and Peter had ever seen. I watched from the sandpit as she crouched down for Daniel to twirl the ring in her eyebrow. She let him add a piece to the mosaic, the very last piece of Thomas's nose. Shiny blue. Dan said something that opened her face in a big happy grin. She said something back. Acid ate my insides.

Come afternoon break I caught him at the water fountain.

'What was that all about?'

'Geroffme,' said Daniel.

'You betta fess up.'

'You're hurting me, Harry.' He hated Chinese burns.

'What was it about?'

'What about?'

'What did the art lady say to you?'

'Oh, her. You didn't need to hurt me, Harry. I'd have told you. She said, did I want to help with the mosaic?'

'After that, dick head.'

'I don't know what —'

'What was the last thing she said?'

'Ouch! Harry, stop it! She said, see you shortly, shorty.'

'Before that.'

'Oh.' Daniel smiled. 'She said I was cool.'

'What did you say to her?'

'I don't know. Lots of things. Harry, that's really hurting.'

Does torture work? It was rubbish on Daniel.

'Dan, what did *you* say that made *her* say you were cool?'

'I asked her how come you smell of sherbet.'

'You winding me up?'

'Honest, Harry, that's what I said.'

What was so cool about that? I left him rubbing his wrist and ran off to catch the guys.

'Yo, Harry!' he shouted after me.

I turned and saw Dan Dan standing by the water fountain, a smile back on his face, his thumbs tucked in his trousers, peeling them down a bit. You could see the tops of his Marks & Spencer pants. That's how cool he was.

I decided to make Stanley swap.

'Only til we get moving,' he said, cheeky monkey. If he'd swapped any more slowly he'd have got cramp.

I swept Stanley's Cheesy Wotsits onto the floor and settled into the seat that should have been mine. Through the window I watched the driver unpacking the boot. He laid out people's bags across the tarmac. Something in the curve of his back reminded me of polar bears I had seen at the zoo. He had one of those blue metal toolboxes. Some tools were too long for the box. I noticed a very large spanner. I watched him repack the boot, one thing at a time.

'Driver's up,' said Stanley. 'You've got to swap back.'

I didn't see why I should, but it was obvious Peter wasn't going to back me up. So I was stuck in the middle, the lads still making stupid guesses. They'd been playing forever and we hadn't left the car park.

'It's a good one,' Peter said. 'Something beginning with D, something human, something horrid, something that says, "I'm in charge today." Something that's first name is Mister.'

A cheer went up and I felt the coach move.

D for Donald? Mr Donald not here! I couldn't believe it! Mr Donald was deputy head. He ran every school trip wearing his I'm-in-charge anorak with extra zips and extra pockets, ticking us all off with his red and black pens on his I'm-in-charge clipboard, to make up for all the days when he wasn't in charge. I stood up and looked around. No sign of Mr Donald! Still, we could always pick him up on the way out of London. I shouldn't get my hopes up.

'Head DOWN in the back,' shouted Mr Pratt from the front. 'QUIET PLEASE.'

He was using Mr Donald's Important Announcement Voice, bashing odd words on the head.

'Okey Dokey! I'm sure you'll ALL be disapPOINTed to KNOW that Mr DONald can't be WITH us on the TRIP.'

Me and Peter started going 'Ahhhh,' and everyone joined in. It was the best news since the cleaning ladies poisoned Mr Donald's gecko.

Terry had no idea about the Mr Donald Experience. I filled him in.

'Gruesome,' he said.

We swung round Shepherd's Bush roundabout. Mr Pratt wobbled on one ginger leg.

'Mr DONald is unwell!' he said.

I hoped it was serious.

Mr Pratt got his balance back.

'So, I'M in CHARGE today!'

We had a good laugh at that one. The little kids laughed along but you could tell they didn't get it. I had a feeling we were going to have a brilliant day. I was about to say so to Piggy, but he was busy shoving his finger up his nose.

'This trip is your reward for fine work!' shouted Mr Pratt.

It was true. The construction teams in my class and Dan's had done an absolutely brilliant project.

'And in return you must remember that you are representing the very best of Mandela School!'

Piggy hooked out a bogey. Peter leaned over and rubbed at something Stan was drawing in mist on the window, something rude.

'So, behave with all the courtesy that would make Mr Mandela proud! That includes you, My Sissay!'

I don't know why he had it in for her. If we ever let girls in the gang, *if* we did, My Sissay might stand a chance.

Piggy munched. I felt a fart coming along.

'The reputation of the school depends on you!'

That's when I let rip a big one.

I was right. It was a brilliant day. As the bus climbed the hill to Legoland, out of the radio came that song about cleaning your teeth and seeing your friends and the sights and feeling aaaall right.

Felt like they were singing about us.

Huge letters of the alphabet made of Lego bricks spelled out L-E-G-O on the grass beside the road. We shouted each letter.

In the car park we got off the bus and had a skipping race to the entrance. Terry won by miles. I beat Peter at the line, but he said I didn't. Stanley was quick. Piggy lumbered in last. I looked back and saw Daniel way behind, bugging the bus driver, asking his usual idiotic questions, most likely.

We rushed through the entrance, clouds moved and sunshine blasted Legoland, lighting up the bright blues and reds and yellows and I felt we really were in another land completely. Everything was made of Lego. Absolutely everything.

Soon as they'd got us through the gates, Mr Pratt and Miss Burton – she was so mousy I hadn't noticed her before – legged it for the café. Mr Pratt called over his shoulder,

'I'll be watching you all from the terrace.'

That wasn't true, because:

A: Legoland was gigantic.

And B: He'd be scoffing bacon baps and teasing Miss Burton about her dangly jangly earrings.

We couldn't believe our luck. Duckshit Donald would have had us synchronising our watches and agreeing to meet up with a designated grown-up at a designated meeting point to get ticked on the I'm-in-charge register every five minutes, I bet.

Dan Dan was hanging around by the Lego shop talking to a dinosaur when we raced for the Hill Train that took us down to the rides. Terry opened his packed lunch and shared out Pringles and fizzy things that make your head explode.

After the Technic Garage – they had a life-size Lego motorbike – me and Peter exchanged our secret signal and nagged at Terry to buy us extra large cups for the Coca-Cola fountain and a Mars Bar each.

'You must be joking, guys,' he said, passing our test with flying colours. We didn't like boys who tried too hard. Pity we missed out on the Mars Bars, though. Piggy bought one for his self and didn't offer us a bite.

Peter got drenched in the Pirate Falls, then Terry showed us how to construct water bombs out of paper from a notepad he'd brought with him. It was like making paper boats only eight hundred times more complicated. We filled them up in the toilets. They were a dead ringer for real bombs, except fatter and made of paper.

'Word of advice, guys, strategy, strategy!' said Terry when Piggy asked why we couldn't launch them straightaway.

'Think stealth. Conserve your ammo. Apply for maximum impact.'

We didn't know what he was on about but it sounded fantastic. I could see Terry wouldn't be spending long in the lower divisions.

We had to queue for ages to get on the Sky Rider. We sweated buckets and Terry's nose turned pink. Peter never burned. His dad came from Goa. Terry was the freckliest boy I'd ever seen. Piggy whined a lot. Stupid, really, when we were trying out a new boy for the gang. Piggy ought to think about his position.

There was room for two boys on each Sky Rider truck and Peter was dissing Piggy for squelching God Save the Queen under his armpit when our turn came – 'That's so immature,' he said – so I slipped past him and got in the first truck with Terry. Peter had to share with Piggy.

'Look!' Peter hissed, as we rounded a bend, 'Dan and Stan!'

Looking down made me feel queasy – I had a problem with heights, but I had a quick shufty. There they were, running along holding hands, like girls, heading into range.

'Wait for it,' Terry ordered. Peter froze in mid throw.

'Don't throw. Drop. But wait for it. I'll give the signal.'

That was a bit off for a new boy. But then again, if it wasn't for Terry we wouldn't have any bombs.

'Bombs away!' he ordered.

We all let go. Had we left it too late? No, we hadn't. Terry's bomb bounced off Stanley's head and burst all over Daniel. Another one, mine I expect, was a direct hit on Stanley.

Stanley went into a screaming, stamping tantrum. Dan glared up, pouting, but when he saw it was us he had a laugh and a wave. For a moment I was proud of him. We glided by. I tried to fix my eyes on the horizon. Didn't want a dizzy spell in front of Terry.

In the Circus tent we saw a magician who was useless. You could see exactly where he'd hidden the chicken and it wasn't a real chicken, anyway. In fact he wasn't a real magician, just a spotty college kid dressed up, I bet. Probably got more Coca-Cola than he could possibly drink and some Mars Bars and free rides at closing time. I decided to get a job at Legoland when I was old enough.

On the way to the dodgems we spotted Stan and Dan at the baby-dodgem Driving School with a load of other kids. They stood in line on a special stage while a Legoland lady handed them licences. Stan had got his already. Come Dan's turn we all shouted and clapped.

Piggy chanted, 'Pick-ulls! Pick-ulls!' the way people do at football matches. We didn't join in. Piggy stopped and went red in the face.

Dan beamed so brightly I said to the guys, 'Dya think he thinks it's a real licence?'

'Dan's not that stupid,' said Piggy, so I gave him a look.

Pete nipped over to give Stanley his lunch box. Would he notice that me and Piggy had eaten his Jaffa Cakes?

It was closing time at Legoland when Mr Pratt counted us onto the bus and told us to sit in exactly the same place as before and to holler if anyone was missing.

'He said the same place,' said Stanley when I ordered him out of the window seat. 'You're in the middle, Harry.'

I looked to Peter for some back-up. He was heads together with Terry, so I settled down, in the middle, again.

'Do I hear a holler?' said Mr Pratt. 'Heads down in the back.'

I leaned over to Stanley. 'Would you like a Jaffa Cake?'

'Oh, yeah!' he said.

'Tough.'

No-one hollered.

'All prrresent and corrrect,' shouted Mr Pratt, and we cheered.

'Okey Dokey!' He clapped his hands. 'We'rrre off!'

I shared out my cheese-spread sandwiches. They were warm and runny and tasted of lunch-box.

'Strange tasting Brie,' said Terry.

'It's not Brie. It's La Vash Key Ree.'

'What's that?' said Peter.

'It's French for The Cow Who Sings.'

'I mean, what sort of cheese?'

'Triangles.'

I could feel more pointless yap coming on, or another game of I Spy, so I snuggled down for some kip.

Terry was going on about his dad's apartment in Los

Angeles with a pool and a tennis court and two servants
with foreign names who did everything for you and you
only had to throw your clothes on the floor and next
morning they'd be washed and ironed, folded up like in
the shops, and Peter kept saying Wow and Cool and
Wicked like he was after an invitation already, and there
were a few scraps round the bus but not on our row. It
was dark outside and suddenly raining hard and the driver
turned off the lights and the heating came on and the
bus smelt of chocolate and sweaty kids and cheese and
onion crisps and it was cosy and warm and the windscreen wiper did its sleepy thing behind us and everyone
settled down in the dark.

A sharp clap woke me up. I stuck my head round into the
next row. Brendan Murphy, the idiot, had blown up a crisp
packet and burst it with a bang. He'd showered himself
with crumbs, served him right. I was going to tell him
off, but a weird kind of excitement buzzed round the bus,
so I said,

'What's up, Scurfy?'

He said, 'Someone's really for it.'

Kylie Kelly leaned over from the window seat, crinkled
her nose and said, 'He don't know zzzip.'

I kept my eyes on Scurfy. 'Who is it?'

He said, 'They're really gonna get it.'

Kylie gave me her told-you-so face, then got her head
over an empty Sainsbury bag like she was going to throw
up. There were holes in those bags — to stop babies suffo-
cating. I could warn her about that. Decided not to.

Nobody knew anything, so I snuggled down and drifted off.

Next thing I knew Kylie was stood in the aisle blubbering to no-one in particular something about Miss Burton.

'I told her I felt sick and she said Not Now Kylie but I told her I should have a front seat I've got a note and everything.'

No sick in the bag. Faking, I bet. She squeezed past Scurfy, got back in her seat, blew her nose and blubbed,

'Miss told me Don't Be So Selfish Kylie Don't You Know That A Child Has Gone Missing.'

Which would explain why Mr Pratt was lurching down the aisle with his finger in the air, counting kids and chewing his lip.

Kylie whined, 'But how should I know? It's not my fault and I do feel sick.'

We moved under some lights. I caught a flash of Miss Burton at the front. Bones stood out in her neck. Her jangly earrings hung like icicles. She was the colour green. Then I myself got a feeling like ice in my belly. I hadn't checked to see that Daniel was aboard.

I decided to take a stroll down the bus.

Kylie called after me, 'Tell Miss I'm gonna throw.'

Fat chance.

Daniel ought to be on the left, towards the front, just ahead of Parimal.

Some people had left bags in the aisle, which were hard to see in the dark. It took me forever to get on. I could still hear Scurfy growling, 'You throw up on me and you're dog-meat, Kylie Kelly.'

I wouldn't have said dog-meat if I was him.

Kylie retched.

Who was that sitting next to Brian Smith? Sandra Michels! Brian, you skinny twat! I'd always thought Brian was nearly premier league, you know, if he put on some weight. Then he goes and blows it sitting next to a girl. If it was all right to sit with girls I might have sat with My Sissay. But it wasn't, not if you were premier league, no way.

I trod on a bag. Something breakable broke under my foot.

Someone grabbed my arm, said, 'Hey, Harry, guess what?'

I said, 'Not now. I'm looking for –'

Was going to say Daniel but it scared me.

William Plumb whined, 'I did go before we came. I did. But now I needs to go again.'

I accidentally knocked Parimal. His Fanta spilt on his trousers. He started crying, the big cry baby. I didn't stop to apologise. Daniel's seat was right in front of Parimal's. Daniel wasn't in it.

A tingle shot down my arms and snapped out of my fingertips. I thought I'd see sparks. I heard the noise of my heartbeat and William Plumb like a scratch on my eardrum going,

'Cross your legs and chew your tongue, she said. That's rubbish and crap, that is, rubbish and crap.'

When my legs worked I moved forward. Two rows along I breathed again. Daniel sat on his own, on the left, near the front, cuddling his anorak.

'Don't worry, Biffo,' he said, 'it's all right, it's all right.'

I don't think I'd ever been so glad to see him. I didn't let on. I said,

'Cheers, big ears. Budge up. What's happening?'

Amazingly, Daniel knew exactly what was happening.

'It's Adrian Mahoney, Harry. He's not on the bus. They thought he was, and then they thought he wasn't and now they've decided he definitely is not on the bus.'

'But –'

'The thing is, Harry, Mr Pratt thinks he might have counted Jason twice.'

Teachers were always getting Adrian and Jason confused. They both had wide blue eyes and floppy blond hair and they both loved skateboards and they argued about who supported Man United the best. (It was Adrian. He had actually been to Old Trafford with his dad.) Miss Bliss, our class teacher, called them the Mahoney twins, but they weren't related. Jason's real name was Smith.

Suddenly, everyone was an expert on Adrian Mahoney.

'He was with a lady and a man,' that smelly girl from Dan's class said over and over again.

'He might have left his bag and gone back for it,' said William Plumb, gripping his trousers.

The driver's huge head bobbed about in a cheerful way. He sang snatches of something he had playing on his head-phones.

It seemed daft to me that the bus was ploughing through the rain on the motorway, what with Adrian miles back in the dark, lost in Legoland, but grown-ups don't ask your opinion when you're nine and a bit and they don't like you to offer it neither.

The driver sang loud and totally out of tune:

'Theeengs,' Bob. Bob. Bob. Bob.

'Are geddin much bedda.'

If he could have heard himself he'd have died.

I went to report my hot new intelligence to the boys at the back and found Scurfy in my seat.

'But Kylie's being sick,' he said when I told him to shift it.

I heard retching.

'Tough.'

The lads were impressed that I knew all about everything. I didn't say Daniel had told me. We instantly came up with millions more ideas than Mr Pratt who was swinging his head about wildly as if Adrian might any second just turn up.

'Strategy, guys,' said Terry. 'We should call the police and go back.'

'Yeah, guys, we should call the police,' said Peter who never said 'guys'. It was Terry's word.

'We'll form search parties,' said Terry. 'We'll need four team leaders.'

'I'll be a leader.'

'No, Harry. We'll need super-fast scouts to keep the search teams in contact. You're the fastest runner we've got.'

I couldn't argue with that. Any minute Terry might disappear behind the seat and spring out dressed as Superman, he was so brilliant at dealing with disaster.

'How come you know so much about it?' said Piggy.

Terry looked around like there might be enemy spies, and growled,

'I shouldn't tell you this but my dad's a big cheese in the SAS.'

'What's the SAS?' shouted Stan, like a moron.

'You seen Thunderbirds on TV?'

Peter's round eyes grew like they'd pop out of his head.

'International Rescue!'

'It's like that,' said Terry, 'only real life and dangerous.'

'My Grampa fought in Spain,' I said.

'Yeah,' Piggy snorted, 'To get his deck-chair first before the Germans nabbed them.'

'He got his eye shot out and won some medals, actually,' I said.

'Wicked!' said Terry.

Terry was most definitely a premier league boy. The way things were going, me and Peter might be battling it out for deputy. As for Piggy, he'd find himself in the relegation zone if he didn't watch his form.

A barf and a wet stink came out of Scurfy's row.

'Miss! Miss! Come Quick!' he shouted.

I put my head round. Kylie was dabbing herself with a tissue.

'I'm all leaky, Miss!'

I could have told her about those holes.

Miss Burton picked her way down the bus, glared at Kylie, and took the bag off her.

Scurfy whined, 'You're drippin on me, Miss.'

Miss Burton didn't hear. She dripped all the way to the front of the bus. Lucky I hadn't left my things in the aisle.

'It's not fair. I've got a note and everything,' Kylie blubbed. 'My jeans!'

'Least it's your own sick,' said Scurfy.

There were sniffer dogs and helicopters with heat-seeking binoculars in our search plan by the time Mr Pratt pulled out his mobile. The way he stared at it you'd think he'd not seen one before. His thin legs trembled. We pulled over at a service station, slowed down and stopped. We all surged forward.

'Not so fast,' said a tight voice through the speakers. 'Sit down and be quiet.'

We all sat down.

'Thank you,' said the voice. It was the driver. Sounded like he was in charge.

I scooted down to sit with Daniel, taking care not to slip on the sick.

'He should have told me straightaway,' the driver said.

Miss Burton nodded like those toy dogs people have in the back of their cars. Her dangly earrings swung like spaniels' ears.

Mr Pratt yelled into his mobile,

'I said L for Larry. Not a town . . . No. Legoland. Near Windsor . . . Hold on. I'm breaking up.'

He really was.

'I'm still here. Are you there?'

Daniel snored.

Mr Pratt scratched the back of one goosebumped leg and shouted into his mobile,

'Look! We've just realised we're one child short!'

That wasn't true. He'd been dithering for miles.

'Adrian Mahoney . . . No . . . Adrian . . . Adrian. A for Apple.' His voice cracked. 'D for Dog.'

Rain thudded on the coach.

It was when he started turning Adrian into some vital statistics, a list of colours and clothing, that I felt seriously nervous. I imagined Adrian soaked through in his Man United strip, squelching round the car park in the black night, searching for our bus. Maybe some nice family had picked him up and taken him home, wrapped him in a fluffy towel and given him some cocoa. Maybe not.

We all knew it was dangerous to be separated from your group, to be alone in the dark, to ask strangers for help. Just walking about in a car park wasn't safe. And right now this minute, probably, Adrian was doing all four things at the same time. Not to mention, he could catch his death of cold. I imagined him riding his skateboard over the tops of some cars, which was the one thing I could think of that could possibly make things more dangerous for Adrian.

'I'm not asking you, I'm telling you,' the driver snapped.

Mr Pratt mumbled something back at him.

It struck me as tough on Mr and Mrs Mahoney if Adrian was dead or lost for good, because there'd always be Jason Smith riding his skateboard in his Man United strip with his hair flopping about, a ghostly Adrian reminding them of what they had lost. Daniel's head dropped against my shoulder. I didn't push him off.

'Let me put it this way,' said the driver. 'If you don't try to contact that boy's parents, you'll be lucky to be teaching safe cycling when all this is over.'

I didn't think he'd be much good at that.

'Are you hearing me, Sunny Jim?'

Mr Pratt started spelling out Mahoney on the phone.

Dan wouldn't know if I put my arm round him. It was more comfortable that way for me. His head slipped onto my chest. He nuzzled against me. It was all right. No-one could see. I looked from Dan's legs to mine. His were delicate and white, with soft baby hair, not like mine at all. His head smelt of clean dog and I liked it.

I must have dropped off too, because I woke up and had to snatch my arm away sharpish.

Mr Pratt's voice shrieked out of the speakers so high and loud it hurt my ears.

'Adrian's safe, children! Adrian's auntie from Windsor picked him up! Mr Donald had the details! Adrian's safe and sound!'

Mr Pratt turned away. From his shoulders I guessed he was crying.

There weren't supposed to be any stops on the way back, but we were at the service station, and what with all the relief, and the rain reminding everyone of their bladders – William Plumb had actually wet himself – it was obvious Mr Pratt would let us off the coach if we whined enough. Everyone started whining at once.

'Okey-dokey, but just five minutes,' he said. Miss Burton touched his arm and whispered something.

Mr Pratt yelled, 'Make sure you stay in pairs and no running in the car park!'

Me and the lads had a pee at the urinals. Mine reached the highest, then Peter's, then Piggy's and last of all Terry's, which surprised me. Peter was on top form, trying to impress Terry, obviously. He found a little pink square with a balloon thing inside. We knew what it was. We pooled the last of our money, except Peter, who was saving up for his holidays, and bought some Coke and Orange Tango and flakes. We decided to share with Peter on account of the condom and because when he did have things he shared them with us.

Back on the bus we held our noses all the way to our

seats to make Kylie feel bad. By the time Mr Pratt did his check and holler routine Peter was turning purple blowing up the condom.

'Tastes disgusting,' he said.

It felt late when we finally swung into the car park. Mr Pratt was bawling at us to pick up our rubbish and take it all home. He said we should give the driver a round of applause. I threw in a Hip Hip Hooray because he was excellent during the Adrian Mahoney Is Lost And Found Again Disaster.

The rain had stopped. I spotted Mo, tall and slim, her arms crossed over her long black raincoat. She had on dark leggings and her crocodile boots. She was easily the best-looking parent in the car park. I nudged Terry.

'See, there. That's my mum.'

Some of the parents sat in their cars with the doors open, smoking. Little grey smoke signals rose into the night. I imagined they were saying,

'We've been waiting here hours, Mr Pratt, you plonker.'

Or worse.

Mo didn't look angry. I knew, because she told me, that when we'd only been at school for the day her heart beat faster at the thought of us. You could see it in the size of her eyes.

Me and Terry and Peter and Piggy were last off the bus. We'd had a brilliant day with no rows or fighting. We'd messed about and got away with it every time. Plus, Terry was terrific and our new friend. I could let him partner me in the three-legged race on Sports Day. But that would be tough luck on Peter. We always did it together. Pete was my best mate and you shouldn't dump your best mate the minute someone new comes along.

Daniel, like an idiot, had left his anorak behind. I was holding it up by the hood so it wouldn't drag in a puddle when I said see ya to the lads and we scattered.

I ran to Mo.

She said, 'Where's Daniel?'

Her eyes x-rayed the anorak like he might be hiding behind it, flickered over my head, scanned the empty bus.

I said, 'Isn't he with you?'

Then, two things happened at once.

Mo's face went thin.

And I knew what adults meant when they said that hearts sank.

3

Daniel believed he and his friend Sailesh could send each other messages through their trainers. I stared down at my Nikes.

'Harry calling Daniel. Do you read me? Harry calling Daniel. Come in, please.'

Pa tugged me closer so the lady could see.

'Just like this one, only smaller,' he said. 'Head up, Harry.'

I got my head up.

'Please, Harry, co-operate.'

I opened my eyes. The lady was called Lorraine. It said so in red letters on her white apron. Pa stood, arms stiff by his sides. He clutched his Biro like a knife.

The Lorraine lady said, 'I shall have to call the supervisor, Sir.'

Her customers were getting restless. You could tell by their shoes. I ran my eyes along them, tried to imagine what the people looked like. Black, scuffed Doc Martens, one of them tapping. High-heeled sandals, strappy ones, white. A pair of those boat-shaped things for old ladies who have trouble with their feet.

'We've seen the supervisor. Head up, Harry. Please, Miss.'

Pa fished in his pocket, pulled out his wallet, took out

Dan's photograph. Mo's library card fell to the floor. I kept my eyes on it. We'd best not leave anything else at the service station.

'Head up, Harry,' Pa said. 'Lorraine, if I may, Lorraine, please. Take a good look at him.'

He handed her the picture.

Lorraine's eyes rolled from grinning Daniel to gloomy me and back again.

Granada, Here to Help, her label said.

Help, then. Help.

Or stop staring.

Enough people had cut me with their eyes: So, you're the boy who didn't check his little brother was on the coach.

'Now I come to think of it I do believe there's a lad the spitting image of this one here over there in the kitchen having a chat with Grumpy Chef.'

Typical Daniel, poking his nose in, asking how the chip fryer worked and did the tomatoes arrive in those water-thin slices or whole, and, if whole, where did they keep the knives, and if a lady cut herself was she allowed home or did she have to stay working and do something that did not involve fingers. Daniel could easily forget about the coach.

'Have you checked the driving machines, Sir? Little boys do get carried away on those.'

That's what she really said.

Pa's Biro broke in his fist.

'My son's been missing three hours and forty-five minutes.'

You could count to twenty in the time it took Lorraine to get it. Dread spread like nettle rash across her face. I picked up the library card.

42

Someone laughed, 'Oooh! You little devil!'

Strappy Sandals gabbing into her mobile, just as I had imagined her.

Bunion Shoes said, 'My tea's going cold if anyone cares.'

Lorraine rose up behind her till and snapped,

'This little man –. I'm sorry, Sir. This man's little boy has gone missing half the night, Madam. Will you shut up and be patient, please.'

Doc Marten stopped tapping. Strappy Sandals clapped her hand over her mouth like she'd bitten her tongue. Bunion Shoes chuntered and walked off with her tray, not paying.

Lorraine handed Dan's picture back.

'I'm sorry,' she said. 'I only wish I could help. You could talk to Desmond, love, on litter patrol. He's got a good eye for faces.'

'We've talked to everyone,' said Pa. 'You're the very last one.'

I remembered that night on the ferry the summer before when me and Dan were too excited to sleep. We climbed on deck with Mo and peered into the dark. The boat moaned and creaked. Spray wet my face, salt got up my nose, my stomach rolled, my legs played tricks on me. I didn't dare look down in case the sea swallowed me.

'Land Ahoy!' Daniel yelled.

He bounced up and down. Mo took hold of his hood like he was a giant yo-yo.

'Home,' she said.

I swung round searching for Ireland. I saw a dark lumpy strip and pinpricks of light. That wasn't Ireland and it wouldn't be until I raced my cousins across the sands to hunt jellyfish and shout at the sea. That lumpy thing was only a glimpse of what we had coming. Same as each time someone said missing or gone, lost or disappeared, seasick sloshed in my belly, but somehow I knew it was going to get rougher than this.

A policeman waved a flashlight and ran across the car park shouting, 'Found Him!'

Pa stopped with a jolt. His mouth dropped open like in a cartoon.

'You've found him, then!' said the policeman.

Pa's mouth slammed shut. He gulped.

'His brother. Only his brother.'

'My mistake, Sir.'

That policeman could have kicked himself, I bet.

You'd think there'd be helicopters casting super-beams over miles and miles of countryside, sniffer dogs and teams of square-jawed men with guns shouting 'Hut-Hut-Hut!'. The motorway stopped, cars searched, drivers spread-eagled, interrogated, frisked.

It wasn't like that.

Beyond the petrol pumps, I could see, I could see but I couldn't believe it, cars pouring back onto the motorway.

At school, when Joshua Bernstein's glasses went missing for the third time in one morning, Miss Bliss made us search the whole classroom. We couldn't find them.

The bell rang for lunch.

Miss Bliss said we should sit with our eyes closed until someone gave them back.

Tummies rumbled.

Miss Bliss said, 'It's chicken stroganoff for lunch.'

Chairs scraped.

'I understand when that runs out there's Mrs Stothard's veggie bake.'

Vomit bake, we called it. Kids nudged other kids.

I peeked and caught Scurfy Murphy slipping his hand inside his book bag.

Miss Bliss said, 'I hear there's apple crumble for dessert.'

Scurfy slid Joshua's glasses case across the table towards My Sissay. As if she had done it! Then, you know what? Well, I'm not going into that now. I mean, the point is, they were only glasses and Daniel was, Daniel.

I wanted Pa to take the policeman and shake him until we got Daniel back. Why didn't they do something? Instead, they wittered over the same old details that had got us, so far, precisely, nowhere.

I tried to take everything in before more cars sped off and disappeared into the night. On a trailer, in front of us, three long rowing boats cut in half. How would they stick them together? A sign on a Toyota Landcruiser said, 'Cambridge University Boat Club.' A baby cried. Someone hoiked and spat. I didn't hear it land. Two motorbikes, Moto Guzzis, ticked. I saw no stars. There was a taste of metal in my mouth. How could the policeman possibly know which of these details were clues?

He was talking to me.

'Pardon?'

'So you didn't see Daniel after you got on the coach, Harry?'

As if I hadn't told them already.

'He's not stupid. He wouldn't wander off on his own.'

Then I remembered, the way Daniel saw it he wasn't alone. He had Biffo with him. Darkness swirled round me. The tarmac sped up towards me, but when it hit me it was soft and warm and smelt of Pa.

Next thing I knew we were driving down a big wide street like Ladbroke Grove, only it was quiet and empty except for one black cab, its top light off and no passengers, seemed like a funeral car, swinging round the corner.

We pulled into a street a lot like our street. I yawned, rubbed my face and saw the pub, the second-hand clothes shop, Alastair's restaurant, the Aids place, like on our street. I didn't get it, never known a morning that didn't have a bedtime first.

By the time I'd worked that out, something else had crept up on me. Daniel had been gone the whole of the night.

Mo tumbled from the house in her leggings and croco-dile boots. Her coat snagged on the roses. She gawked into the car. Me and Pa got out, shut the doors. Mo's face crum-pled. There were no hugs, no words. She turned and walked into the house. Pa followed after.

Felt like the roses holding me back.

'Psssst. I thought you was with Daniel.'

'Oh, yeah. Look who's talking.'

'Kiddo, there's no time for recrimanotwots, OK? I'm here to help.'

That one again.

'I have to tell you, boy, it's time to quit dreamin and be realistic. You gonna need some protection.'

'Look, I'm nine and a bit. I don't believe in crappy invis-ible friends. And if I did –'

'Who are you talking to?'

It was Pa. I told him, Biffo. He shivered, passed a hand in front of my face.

'You're asleep on your feet, honey. Come inside. Just a dream.'

I hoped it was. I had enough on my plate.

4

I woke up and there was Daniel.

I shouted, 'Mo! Pa!' Nothing came out.

I felt the shape of an estate car around me. We sat cross-legged, me and Daniel, in the boot, on the back seat folded flat. In front of us, a cage thing, the sort dog people have.

'Your go, Bro!' I hated it when Dan said that.

We had our jimjam jackets on, that's all. I felt grit under my bum, and in my bones an itch that said I should be doing something. But what? I did my memory trick, sent a search party round my brain. They found a desert that was completely silent, cold and dark and they got lost in it.

'I'm wait-ing.' That annoying singsong way of his.

In my hand was Mr White, the painter, and his family. I must be dreaming. In real life I'd never play Happy Families. All cards with Dan was torture.

'One for me.

One for you, Harry.

One for. Hang on a sec. I'll just take those back and –'

You could murder him.

Dan said, 'What you got?'

He didn't understand the point of keeping your cards to

yourself, had his and Biffo's cards face up. He'd set his out in fathers, mothers, sons and daughters.

'I know it's supposed to be families. I like it this way.'

'But, Dan.' If we could just get on, maybe that itch would go away.

'Dan, even Biffo's got the right idea.'

'Not Biffo,' Daniel whispered. He glanced towards the driver, whose head bobbed about in a happy way.

Outside, red lights trailed into the night. On inky hills, yellow pinpricks flickered. Must be a city. I should be looking out for crooked spires or leaning towers or great gigantic angels. Something, anything, that might say where we were. Instead, I counted cards and wondered if a Chinese burn would help.

'You're a stickler for the rules. Eh, Sunny Jim?' A clear, tight voice cut through the night. Ice dripped down my back.

'Curious . . .'

Twelve cards I had.

'Considering how you yourself respect them.'

Betting on frogs for real actual money. Watching South Park round at Piggy's. Showing Kylie my willy accidentally on purpose that time because of building works we changed for games in class. I had broken lots of rules.

'I think your parents should be told.'

In real life our family believed the only rules that mattered were the ones about not hurting people. This wasn't real life.

'What do you say?'

I felt Dan shiver. We must not let that man hear us, see us, touch us. We must not give that man one word.

He said, 'Let's keep it as our secret.'

I bit my tongue and tasted blood.

'Good, then, I'm glad that's settled.'

I wanted to reach out to Daniel, warm him up a bit. I tried to figure out the something I had to do, but fear and something worse, I couldn't name it, had got hold of me. My legs went warm, then wet, then cold. A dark pool crept out across the gap between Daniel and me.

Everything wrong. Dry mouth, fuzzy tongue, fuzzy teeth, the pillow wet, spicy sheets, my clothes still on. Soaked. Something heavy on my chest, you couldn't see or touch it.

Oh. The bad thing. Pa broke his promise to drive carefully on the motorway.

Oh. The really bad thing.

Daniel. Missing.

Someone didn't check that Dan was on the bus.

Oh.

That someone.

It was me.

Strip off my clothes. Try to poo. Can't do it. Scrub my teeth and tongue. Get the hottest shower I can bear. Step into steam. Squirt lime gel on nailbrush. Scrub. All over. It hurts but I can't feel it. Scrape ears out with fingernails. Breathe hot water through my nose. Blow. Soap my bum. Clench. Pee. Clench harder. Squeeze out the final drop. The slightest trace of Harry.

Kid in the mirror wearing a towel won't look me in the eye.

I can see some things about him.

Scared to be alone.

Wants to cry.

Can't.

'Da-Daaah!'

Sudden weight upon my back. Sticky fingers round my eyes. Cheerio breath in my face.

'Da-Daaah! Guess Who?'

You never had to guess with Daniel. Perched on the stairs above the landing. Same ambush every time.

I might step aside, let him crash into the wall. Or play along if I felt kind. Fight back more often, floor him. Times I really did forget. Not many.

'Da-Daaah! Guess What?'

He couldn't keep a thing to himself.

'Did you see the hillycopters? Can you guess where I was hiding?'

Oh, Dan. I wish.

Everything wrong. Strangers in the living room. A lady and a man. An ashtray on the kitchen table. The morning, dark. Dark, as if it knew.

In the kitchen Mo and Pa so still and grey I hardly notice them at first. Statues.

Mo: coat, leggings, crocodile boots, hair kind of scraggy.

Pa: gardening cords, checked shirt, inside out, dressing gown. Hasn't shaved.

Pa to me: 'Baby, what happened to your skin?'

The phone.

Mo, Pa, jolt as if connected.

The phone. Mo to Pa, a mighty effort: 'You.'

The phone. Pa dives and picks it up. The stranger lady hovers at the door.

'Oh. You . . . No. Nothing. Thanks . . . We will.'

'You'll catch a chill.'

Pa takes off his dressing gown and wraps it round me. Funny kind of smell on it.

'It's dark, Pa.'

'No more than usual.'

'The morning's never dark.'

'It's evening, Harry.'

'How?'

'We let you sleep, darling.'

'What day?'

'Today is Monday.'

Saturday, wedding. Sunday, Legoland.

'Monday?'

'Monday, honey.'

Monday, nearly gone.

Pa: 'Must eat.'

The clock says half past eight. I didn't know it was the ticking kind. No tocks.

Pa: 'Must eat.'

Quarter to nine.

I watch the big hand clicking round.

53

Just after nine Pa takes an egg and stares at it. He breaks the egg into a bowl, another egg, another. He whisks, six eggs altogether, a lot of shell. He finds a pan, fires the gas, pours oil, pours eggs, then stirs.

Tick. Tick.

Nine fifteen Pa opens windows for the smoke, scrapes burnt egg mush in the bin, wipes his sleeve across his face and weeps.

'It's only stupid eggs, Pa.'

Nine-thirty or thereabouts Pa gets three bowls, serves cornflakes, opens the fridge and yelps,

'No milk.'

'I'll get it, Pa.'

Two semi-skimmed and Dan's full cream stand on the doorstep. I take the semis. Warm.

'Pssst! You give some thought to my suggjestion? . . . Naah? Big surprise . . . Whatsamadda? Think cus I'm invisible I'm no good?'

'You didn't check,' I want to shout. 'You didn't check. You didn't check and holler.'

Instead, I say, 'He never said you were a Yank.'

'You never asked him. As I remember it, you thought I was a figment of his imaginings.'

I turn away and push the door.

'Waid a seggund. I don't wanna debate you, Kid. That aint why I'm here. I'm kinda troubled too, you know?'

I don't give a monkey's for his troubles. I'm through the door.

'Kiddo? Fact is, we didn't check. Here. Come back. I wanna show you something. There.'

Dan's bottle on the step.

'See this?'

It shakes and wobbles, then, explodes.

'You see?'

I saw.

'I can help you, Kid.'

Pa comes and takes the semis from my hands.

'No matter, Harry. I can't manage three. Look at the size of me.'

He's smaller than before.

Munch.

Me and Pa eat cornflakes.

Munch.

Mo slides her spoon about – Dan's trick.

The stranger lady, Wendy, from the police, wants a little word. Pa says would I like to put some clothes on first.

No. Pa's dressing gown and the towel will do fine for now.

I sit on the leather sofa next to Wendy. She has her note-book open on her lap, a mug of hot tea in her hands. She has no uniform and no handcuffs. She won't need them. I'll go quietly.

The other side of Wendy, on the black director's chair, sits a man, very tall, his legs all angles. I forget his name. He has a notebook and a pen. He hasn't got a uniform or handcuffs and he hasn't got a mug of tea. In my memory he hasn't got a face.

Mo and Pa sit on the opposite sofa, one at each end.

Between them a pile of cushions like a mountain. Pa has a mug of tea. Mo couldn't hold one if she wanted to. Claws for hands. She stares ahead. Something odd about her eyes.

Wendy's going on about who she is and why we're here, and then, for no reason, she says,

'If I knocked over this beaker and broke it, then told your mummy that you did it, what would I be doing, Harree?'

'That's my hippo mug!'

She looks at it.

'My favourite!'

'I'm not really going to break it, Harree.' The stupid way she says my name.

She swigs her tea, pretends it hasn't burnt her mouth, places my hippo mug, gently, on the floor.

'Let's forget the beaker, Harree. Let's try it this way. Do you understand what it means to tell the truth?'

Course I do.

'Harree. The truth. Can you explain?'

Coming into our house! Threatening to smash my hippo mug! Calling me a liar! You know the kind of grown-up has a different voice for kids? That's Wendy. I make her wait.

She gets a tissue out and dabs her mouth.

'Can you explain, Harree? In your own time, can you?'

'The truth is saying what happened and not telling lies.' About my hippo mug, for instance.

'Very good. And can you tell me, in your own words, Harree, what you understand as the point of this inter-view?'

She has that face on: you can trust me, I'm a grown-up.

'Looking for Daniel Pickles, Miss.'

'Yes,' she says. 'I think you're very brave.' Lie number one.

'Now, we're moving on to the interview itself. Try to tell me, in your own words, from the beginning, Harree, what happened.'

I tell her everything. About the Sky Rider and the condom and the Jaffa cakes, Adrian Mahoney Lost and Found, the ticking Moto Guzzis, Scurfy Murphy and the sick.

The tall man scribbles in his notebook.

When I've finished Wendy says,

'Excellent.' Lie number two. I knew it had come out all wrong.

'Tell me, Harree, at the service station, do you remember seeing Daniel at all?'

I wonder about her bazongers. Do they have special bras for policewomen?

'Harree?'

Navy ones, thick straps? Extra padding in case of riots?

'At the service station? Did you see Daniel?'

'I told you, no.'

'And when you got back on the bus. Think back, Harree. Did you see Daniel at all, in the car park?'

'I didn't look. It was the condom.'

Mo blinks twice. I see what's odd about her eyes. They've stopped reflecting light, that's what.

'Tell me about the driver, Harree, anything at all.'

I look down as if from an aeroplane on the sofa's leather landscape, tiny criss-crosses of roads, impossible to navigate.

'The driver, Harree?'

If you stuck to the big creases you might be all right.

'Take your time,' she says.

What she means is, 'Hurry up.'

In from the night comes a sad soft voice. 'Sebby, sweet-pea. No games tonight. Please, baby.'

'Polar bears.'

'What?'

'At the zoo, Miss. Have you seen the way . . . It doesn't matter.'

'It does, it does, Harree. What was it about polar bears?'

'You know the way their back goes when they bend? He was big like that. Strong looking.'

She nods at me like she's interested. In polar bears. I mean, come on.

'Anything else? About the driver?'

'He likes D:Ream.'

'Beg pardon?'

'He likes D:Ream. You know.'

She's nodding like a moron.

'*Things can only get better.*'

Mo gulps so hard it sounds like someone pulled the plug out.

'He had it on his headphones, Miss. The song, I mean.'

'Did you say anything to him, Harree?'

'Hip hip hooray, Miss. When we did the clapping.'

'Did he speak to you, Harree?'

'I don't think he knew it was me. He spoke to Dan, though.'

I might have forgot to mention it before.

'That's why Daniel wasn't in the skipping.'

I'd told her about the skipping.

'At Legoland, Miss.'

The tall man stops writing and looks up from his notes. They do some eye talking.

'Harree, let's try concentrating on the driver. From the beginning.'

I do. The tall man scribbles hard.

When I'm done, the lady says, 'Now, Harree, is there anything else you want to tell me? Anything you want to ask?'

I follow one zigzaggy road, maybe a stream, across the leather landscape.

'Anything at all?'

'I'm sorry, Miss.'

'For what, Harree?'

'Not checking, Miss. I should have checked that Dan was on the bus.'

There.

The silence stretches out.

'I want to tell you something, Harree. We all have our jobs to do. I'm a police officer. Your father's a doctor, your mother here's a . . .' she checks her notes, 'a colourist, and you are a boy. A kind boy. A clever boy, I'm sure. But just a boy. It's not your job to be responsible for other people's lives.'

'She's right, Harry.'

That's Pa. I notice Mo has nothing to say about it.

I don't believe Wendy for a minute. She knows nothing about me. I have lost count of her lies. That probably isn't even her own name.

5

It was the kind of day so hot you could see air wobbling up off the black road. We trudged past Parimal and his mum by Noddy's van at the school gates. They stared into their ice-creams. You could tell they weren't really looking. Parimal's ran like sour milk onto the path. It was the Friday after the Friday after the Sunday we lost Daniel. An awful lot of days. Maybe, like some other people, they were having trouble seeing us. Or maybe they felt embarrassed we'd caught them scoffing Noddy's, which we weren't supposed to on account of Miss Burton had a homemade ice-cream stall in aid of the trampoline.

Balloons and bunting fluttered in the trees. The other side of the school the steel band played, *Hap Hap Happy Holidays*. Pa stood, eyes closed, under the hot sun. A moan came out of him. Must have forgotten it was Sports Day.

'Pa.'

You could see the shall-we-shan't-we in his shoes.

'Pa. Miss Bliss will be waiting, Pa.'

He looked at me, blank-eyed, pushed his hands deep into his pockets, leaned forward and launched himself like he was marching into a blizzard. I caught him by the bike sheds where Steven Hickey and Rowan Field shook tins for library books. They stopped shaking as we walked by. Rowan bent down, adjusted his Nikes, the sort you pump with air to make them fit. Steven rubbed his nose and blinked up at the sun.

Pa said, 'Hello, Steven.'

'Ah, hello there, Dr Pickles,' he said like he'd only just spotted us.

Then, starting with his neck, he turned red all the way up to his eyebrows. I'd never seen anyone do that. He didn't say hello to me, but that was all right because he was in top class and I wasn't. The second we got past them they started whispering.

It might have been our clothes they were on about. Pa had on his gardening cords, his winter shirt, his dad's old heavy cardigan. I was in my tracksuit bottoms and my wedding shirt I'd got out of the dirty washing.

I watched our reflection growing bigger in the sign that said, 'Mandela School. A Safe and Happy Place to Learn.' Reminded me of those history pictures of soldiers coming back from the war. Hunched and unhappy, leaning on their pals, bits of them bandaged or missing, their uniforms torn. Looked like they needed their mummies, not like heroes at all.

School's locked on Sports Day. So we had to turn left at the sign, walk around the school, along the path that edged the playing field where happy families in summer shorts and vests and stuff were having fun.

Over where the band was playing, people swayed. The tannoy buzzed.

'Would all sack race contestants gather BEHIND, repeat BEHIND the line.' Mr Donald was in charge.

Dan believed he'd win the sack race. I was glad because it wasn't cool to have a brother who was completely crap at sport.

'What you do is, right,' he said, so excited I thought he'd have a wheezing fit. 'What you do is, you stick your feet right into the corners of the sack.'

That old trick.

I really had perfected a Top Secret Technique, for the three-legged race. Me and Peter had been practising it like mad. What you do is, right, forget that stuff about keeping your leg tight against the other person's, and saying, Right Left Right Left Right Left. Forget your legs. Just hurl yourselves forward at the shoulders. Let the legs do their thing. It's brilliant! Unbeatable! We reckoned it would even beat Cameron and Fergus McNally who won every year because they're identical twins and so they'd originally had only one brain.

'SACK RACE conTESTants. NOW, please.'

William Plumb ran in the wrong direction, his mum tripping after in stupid high heels.

'But I needs to go now,' he shouted back at her.

'You'll have to go in the trees, then, or you'll miss it.'

It wouldn't matter. Dan said William Plumb was crap at sack racing. He ducked under the willow trees just behind where Mousy Miss Burton, sun block on her nose, slopped out organic ice-cream. She had four varieties, all of them horrible. That's why they had to make the rule about Noddy's.

'SACK race PEOple, NOW,' yelled Mr Donald. You wouldn't think it was meant to be fun.

William Plumb scrambled out from under the trees and pulled his shorts up. His mum tugged leaves and stuff out of her hair. Pa plodded on. A man nearly pushed us off the path. He'd yank that girl's arm out if he wasn't careful, that smelly girl from Dan's class.

She said, 'I told you we'd be late.'

He said, 'Don't. Tell. Me. Nuffink. Gel,' like he was a villain off *EastEnders*.

She broke away, ran for the starting line, passed My Sissay sprinting in from the field, all pink and panting in her flashing-light trainers.

'I won the sixty metres, Harry! Won this!'

Gold medal, champion's ribbon attached. So what?

Over her shoulder, far away at the starting line, thirty-two kids in sacks wriggled like maggots. Thirty-two minus Dan, in fact. Minus that girl as well, probably. I felt a bit sorry for her. One whole entire minute before the start of each event Mr Donald disqualified latecomers whatever their excuses so they'd be grateful to him in adult life. Her, me and Daniel, all in Leonardo House, making zero contribution to points this year. Pity, that.

'I said BEHIND the LINE, Stanley Pacheko.'

Pushy little Stan, down the back with the big boys when he should have been up front with Dan, checking and hollering that Dan wasn't aboard.

'It's for you,' said My. 'Take it.'

I'd forgotten she was there, and now I remembered I could think of nothing to say. Between us stood an invisible wall made of kryptonite, wide as the school, high as the sky. On her side kids ran races, won medals. On my side little brothers disappeared. She shoved both hands through the wall – you'd think she'd break her wrists off – pushed the medal into my hand, and ran, red lights flashing all the way to the ice-creams.

'Sweet of her,' said Pa.

I had no pockets, stuffed the medal down my sock.

Maybe a note had gone round telling people to be nice to me like when Bradley Parker's dad fell off the scaffolding and we all wrote saying sorry your dad's dead even though Bradley wasn't in our class and no-one liked him anyway.

'On your MARKS, get SET.'

Crack! Pa jumped so fast, seemed like the gun had shot a bullet through him.

Thirty little maggots wriggled up the field. We watched, as if from a far, cold planet, heard happy voices urge them gently on and Oscar Harding's mother shrieking,

'Jump, Oscie! Jump!'

That girl had actually made it. She was doing really well, might even win it. I don't know. Before the end Pa sulked off. I caught him by the staff room window, saying, 'Excuse me, please,' to that girl's dad who flicked at his lighter, blocking the path with his rude elbows, his back turned on the field. Didn't give a monkey's that his kid had maybe won the sack race. Not a monkey's. She should have disappeared instead of Daniel.

The band was doing *Island in the Sun*. Parents wiggled their hips. Some looked quite cool. Kylie Kelly's mum jerked her hands above her head and really started grooving. Big mistake. Kylie saw us, giggled, slipped behind her mum. You could have hid a bus back there.

Kylie had her Einstein house sash on, which was a laugh, her being so thick and everything. On her letter to Bradley, Kylie drew a coffin on a cloud.

'It's floating up to heaven, Miss.'

'I think Brad might find this a little – disturbing,' said Miss Bliss.

'But, Miss, it took me ages to do the colouring.' In little dots, with all her felt pens, she'd spelled out 'Daddey' on the lid.

We reached my classroom door. Miss Bliss opened it and drew us in. It felt dark and cool and quiet in there. Smelled of kids and old bananas. She had on a yellow summery dress, the kind a girl might wear. She said, 'Hello stranger,' knelt down, held me by the arms, studied me, not, So, you're the boy, a nicer kind of look. If I could I would have jumped into her eyes.

She seemed different from before. Maybe it was the being up close to her that did it. She had, you know, like she was starting a moustache. I smelt her sweat. Not stinky. Warm and safe. Her knees creaked as she got up to shake Pa's hand. She held it, called him Dominic, took special care with all her words, as if Pa was a bomb, one clumsy move might set him off. I can't remember what she said just then but it was kind.

Pa's gaze drifted off towards the window.

'I have Daniel's artwork here, as well as Harry's, to save you traipsing about,' said Miss Bliss, a bit too loudly. 'I've brought a bag for you, Dominic. Don't worry about return-ing it.'

Pa moved towards the window like a robot.

Crack! The gun for big girls' relay. Pa's head bumped the Hoberman Sphere Miss Bliss had hanging from the ceil-ing. He looked almost his normal height again.

Miss Bliss said to his back,

'It's brave of you to come today.'

Pa shrunk. 'To be honest, we forgot.'

He didn't watch the relay. He'd locked his eyes on one happy section of the crowd where mums and dads fussed kids who'd done the sack race.

'Miss Duncan wants you to know that Daniel did another admirable term's work,' she said. 'He's loved at this school, I'm sure you know that. He's in my prayers. I know you Pickleses don't believe . . .'

Acid chewed my innards.

'As for this one, I was going to say I'll really miss him.'

Go on, Miss, say it.

'But I'm going up a class too. There've been some changes to accommodate Ewan Pratt's suspension. So, Harry, you'll have to tolerate me for another year.' She touched my cheek. 'I will give you all the support that I can.'

People had been saying stuff like that since Legoland. Not to me, though.

Pa sloped back like someone hypnotised and loaded artwork in the bag. Miss Bliss went on about my satisfactory progress in maths – I could do bases and everything, my brilliant English, my splendid art.

'There's an example on display,' she said.

My egg-shell mosaic of a lion, glistening. Sixty-one individual pieces, that took, two coats of varnish. A masterpiece.

Pa zipped the bag.

Miss Bliss told the top of his head, 'It's all here in the report.'

The most fantastic report ever in the history of school reports, with Miss Bliss's impossible to read, Emanuela Balisciano, at the end.

Pa took it, scrunched it, crammed it in his trouser pocket.

A cheer went up. You couldn't tell who'd won the big girls' relay. Einstein, head to head with Mrs Pankhurst at the tape.

Three-legged boys lined up in the distance as Miss Bliss saw us out. I looked for Peter in the crowd. Shame he'd miss his medal. He'd be all right about it. He'd understand that no way could I just carry on like Sports Day mattered.

It wouldn't be right, would it? Not unless there was an emergency. Say, someone from Leonardo relay team broke his leg and they needed a fast, last minute replacement, really urgent, and there was nothing else for it and Mr Donald put out a special request over the tannoy for an emergency substitute to save the day for all the parents, well, then I might run, if it was OK with Pa. I had my trainers on, as it happened. Otherwise, just for the three-legged race, it wouldn't be right, would it? I didn't like to check with Pa in case it was so not right that only thinking it meant I didn't care enough about Daniel.

'I want to watch, Pa.'

'OK. Whatever.'

He put the bag down, seemed to sink into the ground with it, dragged a slow hand across his face. Looked like his dad last time we saw him, only Grampy was ninety-two, and lying down and dead.

The McNally twins, smug as could be, did practice trots before the start – to intimidate the opposition. Piggy had paired with Brian, the skinniest boy in the world.

'BEHIND the line, repeat, BEHIND the line.'

Brian was bent over, messing with the tie or something.

Crack!

Piggy flopped over Brian and landed with a snap. Cameron and Fergus shot off like always, surged towards us. You could believe they still had one brain between them.

Back at the start, Brian screamed and rolled about, clutching his leg.

Parents roared and whistled.

Two dads hauled Piggy off.

That's not what people were shouting about.

Up the field, a tight, strong, pumping machine hurled themselves forwards, gaining on the twins.

First time in Mandela history anyone had got close to them.

Cameron swung round, lost his timing, tipped Fergus off balance.

Cameron tripped and recovered and tripped and they were blaming each other before they crashed into the ground.

The crowd whooped and clapped. The pumping machine powered across the line.

Peter and Terry. It was Peter and Terry. Tangled in tape.

Peter and Terry hugged like they'd won the Olympics.

Peter spotted us. Joy froze on his face. He moved towards us, Terry held back, Pete stumbled, and the winning machine was just a pair of boys again. They whispered to each other, wheeled round and trotted off in perfect time to get their medal.

*   *   *

I plodded after Pa through the heat. One of the mothers, I don't know whose, smiled to herself, sang that song, *Walkin on Sunshine*, under her breath with the band, moved her shoulders, jutted out her chin with the beat.

'And I feel so good!'

Pee stink rose like steam from my shirt. I thought of those scary people we had seen under Waterloo Bridge when we went to the Irish festival at the South Bank. Dan wasn't scared. He goggled at this lady who was funny in the head and said,

'I think you stink,' with all the hand signals.

I laughed.

Mo grabbed us by the wrists, marched us towards the river, stopped, turned and bent down so she could do that quiet, breathy shout of hers right in our faces.

'We Never Ever Talk To, Or About, Anyone Like That. Do You Hear Me?'

In the middle of the river, on a rusty barge, a man in a donkey jacket hauled rope.

'Well Do You Harry?'

'Yes, Mo.'

'But she does stink,' said Dan.

'And So Would You Daniel Pickles Had You Nowhere But A Cardboard Box To Lay Your Head.'

I'd bring my torch, have midnight feasts, adventures in the dark.

'In the Cold and the Damp with Spiders and Rats and Nothing to Eat But Other People's Leftovers. No Treats, Ever.'

Oh.

'You Don't Know How Lucky You Are Boys.'

'But, Mo –'

'But nothing, Harry. Life throws all sorts of horrors at people and some people fall down and find it hard to get up again. We are very fortunate to have the life that we do.'

She let that sink in.

'Now.' She let go our wrists, straightened up, got her breath back. 'You know exactly what's required of you.'

We shook on it.

'Sorry, Harry.'

'Sorry, Daniel.'

Dan smiled.

'Not That!'

'Mo, you can't be serious!'

'You don't know how serious I am, Harry Pickles.'

She made us do it. She marched us back and made us actually apologise to the bag lady.

St Patrick's Day, that's all, not long ago, and here we were on Sports Day, box people already, down and smelly and Daniel gone, and I felt we would never get up again.

6

I imagined Otis and Joan, full of honeymoon, catching sight of his mum among the happy people in Arrivals. Small and neat, her hands resting on her tummy, she'd have on her usual Sunday get-up, the white blouse and navy skirt, the shiny-buttoned blazer, her hat, and, hanging off her elbow, that weightlifter's handbag she lugged about everywhere.

'Hooray!' they'd think. 'What a triffic surprise! But she shouldn't have gone to the trouble.'

Then they'd see her, really see her. She wouldn't be smiling.

Would she come right out and say it?

'Daniel's gone. It's Harry's fault.'

Probably not.

Funny, the way she stood on tippy-toes to give our gigantic Otis that little boy's hug. She was his mummy still. She'd do her best to put it gently.

'The thing is, dears, little Daniel has been gone as long as you have, almost. No, he's not on his holidays. No, dears. He's been mislaid in a car park.'

Crouched behind the banister rails, trying to make myself small – my heart might rip out of me it was thumping so hard – I wiped my hands on my boxers, scared they of all people would look at me thinking, So, you're the boy.

Mo clung to Joan like she was drowning. Otis held Pa like he'd got a huge baby to burp. I tried to magic them back onto the dance floor, coloured lights, mushy music, the couples swapped about, that's all, Mo in slinky silver, not her dressing gown, shaking with laughter, not screaming and dribbling.

Otis spotted me. I drew back. He put Pa down, came to the bottom stair, held out his arms. With his eyes he said, 'Come on, I'm waiting,' so I jumped, from the fifth, same as always, and, same as always, he caught me.

He carried me through to the patio, sat on the low wall. I wrapped my legs round him. Calm rose like Vick's VapoRub off Otis's chest. Sure as if I'd been coshed from behind, I went blank.

I must have slept and stayed sleeping while Joan made us tea and brought our mugs out, and the tea Joan had made us turned bitter and cold. When I came to I was howling, great jerking sobs, weeping snot on his shirt.

'Let it go. Let it out. Let it go,' Otis hummed.

It seemed to come with his heartbeat, steady and strong. I clung on til I had cried myself out and those shuddering after-shocks rolled in.

'Good man. Well done, Harry. Good man.'

I only moved when I had to, on account of pins and needles in my legs. Otis unwound me, stood me in front of him, gave me his hanky. I blew and gave it back to him. He found a clean bit, blew into it, with the back of his hand wiped his eyes. They were red-rimmed and wet. Otis sniffed. He took a golden package from the Duty Free bag on the wall.

74

'For you, mate.' His fireman voice almost back.

I didn't take it. Otis waited, kept his eyes fixed on mine.

There was something I'd been needing to ask, but it was dangerous, might do Daniel harm, like in *Peter Pan* when children don't believe in fairies. I didn't dare ask it even in my head.

There was a pebble at my feet. I dribbled it round Otis, chipped it, a sweet, David Beckham chip, perfectly timed for Michael Owen, who reads it, chests it, rockets it into the rosebed. Goal!

I turned to Otis. 'Have you got a present for Daniel?'

He didn't blink. 'We have, mate.'

'Maybe I should wait, then. Til Dan's back.'

Otis put the present down, sipped his cold tea, gazed over at the estates as if the perfect reply might be up there in giant letters on the tower blocks. I counted his bristles, reached twelve and gave up. He mustn't have shaved since Barbados. Along the ridge of his nose skin peeled. He seemed darker than when he had left, a smooth, chocolaty dark that turned the roses behind him a deeper shade of red. I was about to ask him how come black people peeled when I remembered my dangerous question still hanging.

'Babe, your sister's on the phone,' Joan said from the doorway.

Otis said, 'I'll call back, babe.'

He put his mug down, held out a hand. Mine disappeared into his.

'I think you should open your present, mate.'

He was silent so long I thought he was leaving it there.

'Open your present. If Daniel comes back there'll be more presents for everyone.'

75

He had both my hands in his hands now. I wanted to shrink, get my whole self in there.

'But, you know, Harry, he's been gone a long time. Two weeks is a very long time for a little boy to be gone. It's possible he won't come back, Harry.'

I tried to snatch my hands away. Otis held on.

'It's also possible that someone took Daniel and hurt him, maybe hurt him very badly, maybe . . .'

I'd clapped my hands over my ears, shut my eyes tight, tight, by the time he actually said it. I hated Otis. For maybe two whole entire minutes I hated him. I wouldn't look at him but I knew he watched me as every second of my hatred ticked away.

When I could just bear the sight of him he was sipping his tea. He held the mug in both his hands and offered it to me. I cupped my hands round his, took one lonely sip. It had nothing to do with the tea. I had my own and it was horrible.

'Now, open your present.'

It felt like a dare. I didn't want to take it. But the crackling and tearing got me excited, same as always.

A T-shirt! A mischievous boy on the front, a cartoon boy with a red and white spotted handkerchief for a hat that was actually a piece of cloth sewn on, not printed. In crazy letters it said,

'Born to be Wild! Barbados.'

I stripped off Pa's T-shirt, pulled on my new one.

'It's fantastic! Just what I wanted.'

That wasn't me being polite. I wanted Otis to ask me why, why was it just what I wanted, so I could tell him about that boy, you know, who forgot to check and everything,

76

that I'd put him behind me and I was a better boy who didn't make mistakes, who needed clothes of his own so he didn't have to keep wearing that old stuff and being reminded of the bad thing that other boy had done.

Otis looked drained all of a sudden, grey under the eyes, so what I said was,

'You'll be in big trouble if you don't call your sister.'

We picked up the mugs and stuff and walked into the house like men, not sniffing or anything.

Joan sat on the leather sofa, doing elephant roars into a bunch of tissues – you'd have laughed another time. She touched my cheek. Her face was puffy.

'I was thinking about staying the night with you guys. Is that OK with you, Harry?'

'What about Otis?'

'On duty, mate,' he said.

'You won't leave us again, will you, Otis?' It just tumbled out.

Otis and Joan could have whole conversations without opening their mouths. They had one of those. Then Otis crouched in front of me and said,

'I'll never leave you, Harry. I'm here for the duration.'

Otis was so fantastic I sometimes forgot that Joan was my auntie long before he sprinted into our lives.

Once, Mo left me for two whole days and two nights and in the end it was me who had to sit for hours in a hot car to go and see her. And when she saw me again, after all that time and my terrible journey, all she could say was,

'Harry, darling! Come and meet your little brother!' She was cuddling a baby.

What happened next was not fair at all.

I stroked its head because she said I could. I found a soft bit and said,

'Look, Mo, it goes in.'

'Harry! No!' she snapped.

Pa yanked me away and fuss fussed over the baby.

'He's all right, it's OK,' he kept saying as if I'd nearly killed it.

A lady, in a uniform, with an upside-down watch, poked her head in, said she'd heard the commotion and, Was Baby All Right?

They all started speaking in code.

Yap, yap, they said. Fonty Nell. Fonty Nell.

It wasn't right, ganging up like that the other side of the bed.

The lady turned to me and said in a loud silly voice, 'Doesn't Baby look like Daddy?'

That wasn't true! I looked like Pa. That baby looked like Mr Potato Head.

Yap, yap, they said. Baby's skin tone. Baby's feeding.

I wondered what that handle was for doing on the side of the bed.

Yap, yap. Baby's wind. Baby's poo.

The bed dropped. Just a little bit.

Mo yelled, 'No, Harry!'

Her skin turned grey. She clutched herself. That baby cried.

Footsteps pounded the corridor.

A man shouted, 'Help! We need a care assistant! My baby's been sick!'

78

The lady gave Mo a secret smile and shot off.

Pa said in a low, angry voice, 'I've had just about enough of it.'

Mo stroked his face. 'Dom, really. Everything's fine. Harry, love, there's something in that drawer for you, a surprise, a little present.'

Pa said, 'I hardly think . . .'

The surprise was it wasn't Action Man.

Mo said, 'Play Dough.'

Pa said, 'It's from the baby.'

Obviously, it wasn't.

I clenched my fists and crossed my eyes and held my breath, which was a trick I'd invented for being good when it was difficult.

Pa said, 'Whatever you're doing, Harry, stop it.'

I stopped just like he told me to and badness whooshed into me just like I knew it would. Off flew the Play Dough.

'Quick, Dom, get a cloth!'

'It was a Accident!'

Pa said, 'We've got to nip this in the bud.'

Before I found out how that felt, Joan breezed in, wearing her uniform, with her upside-down watch, looking very important.

'Hello my Darling Big Boy!'

It was me she'd come to see.

'I want to show you off to my mates. Is that OK with you, Harry?'

It was very OK.

We walked through eight miles of corridors and rode six or ten lifts. I pressed all the buttons.

Everywhere we went people said things like,

'What a handsome boy! Is he yours?'

And Joan said, 'Yes, he is handsome,' and, 'Wish he was mine.'

She showed me off to her friends in broken bones. I saw an x-ray of someone's leg with nuts and bolts in it. A doctor let me play with his stethoscope, which Pa never did because It Wasn't A Toy. A nurse gave me a special pen. There was a KitKat on her desk. I let her play with my Play Dough. She gave me the KitKat. An old lady asked me to do a squiggle on her plaster, and everyone was very impressed that I could write my own name.

'You don't need to do that, Joanie.'

Mo, stick thin in her dressing gown, such weight on her you'd think the doorway she was leaning on might crack and buckle, bring the whole house tumbling down.

Joan looked up from her scrubbing, her tan fading already.

'Ah, no bother, Mo, I . . .'

Mo sagged and sloped off.

'Come on, H. Work to do.'

Before, you know, I'd have found some excuse, but I was glad to help Joan. It was nice to have something to do. She poured bleach, handed me the brush, went back to her scrubbing. I turned my head away, held my breath, reached out and brushed actually inside the toilet.

'Harry, is Mo usually in bed this time of the day?'

'What time is it?'

'About three. The toilet won't bite you, darling.'

Doors opened and shut. Otis and Pa back from the supermarket.

I scrubbed harder. Real bits of actual dry poo came off. It wasn't as bad as you'd think. There's something good about getting things clean.

'The thing is, Auntie Joan.' That brought a shiver on. I sounded just like Daniel. 'I don't really know. The days get kind of squashed together.'

'Does she spend much of the day in bed, do you think?'

Joan, talking quietly, about my Mo. Felt like secrets. We weren't supposed to have those. I scrubbed under the rim, like they say in the ads. How could I tell her the truth about Mo?

'Joan, the world's upside-down. She's let us run out of vitamins and Cheerios and sugar and juice. The bread has gone blue. Shy Geoffrey came round on bin-day, took the rubbish and left me a splintery old cricket bat. What's that all about? People bring puddings, trifle and apple cake and tiramisu. I've been eating dessert, Joan, until I get sick. In fact there's sick in the U-bend. In the kitchen sink, stinking. There's smelly dry poo in the toilet downstairs. It's been there for days, Joan. Not mine. I can't poo any more. Just pee, in the night, every night.'

I couldn't tell her all that. It might be letting Mo down. So I told her something else that had been bothering me, the scary thing I had been keeping from Mo and from Pa and from Wendy who phoned Pa now and then to see if I'd remembered anything new.

I said, 'Joan, Bang Bang's disappeared. It wasn't me this time.' She didn't look scared. Maybe she didn't hear me.

Pa plodded up the stairs. Otis called after him about where to put the washing.

This wasn't my Pa, who saved lives and had ideas about

everything. It was a different Pa, who had trouble hanging socks and needed telling what to do.

How had we got here? Stink and mess. Time all mucked up. The whole beat of our lives lost without Daniel. He was only a boy. It wasn't as if he did any housework.

Joan sloshed another jug-load of water round the bath. I closed the toilet lid, put the bleach bottle on top.

'That's what Mo does,' I said. 'Cos if you pooed in the bleach it'd splash up and burn your bum.'

Joan pulled a hairy lump from the plughole. Maybe some of Dan's were in there and we should save it for evidence. I didn't say that, though. Joan was crying already. She needed a cuddle. I would have done it, but I'd forgotten how.

After tea I ate one whole raw carrot and drank, felt like, eight pints of water, then lapped the square four times with Otis and did my stretching exercises like he said. I didn't ask why. That was the thing about Otis. It was easy to do what he told you. During the stretching I farted like crazy. He didn't mind. Later on I had my first poo in days. It hurt like hell and there was blood.

That night I curled up tight in bed.

'Faith, Kid, you gotta have faith,' said Biffo, over and over like a lullaby.

Up from the square came, 'It's late, Sebastiano. Pleeeeeese.'

I wondered if Shy Geoffrey might have an aluminium baseball bat or a pair of in-line skates he wasn't using any more. Things were getting better. Not much, but they were getting better. I could almost begin to believe that Daniel might come home.

Summer holidays

7

'Howzat!' Cal screamed. It seemed an invitation from another world, the happy world. Come out to play! Half the summer's gone. Go on, mate, come!

I stirred my Cheerios and started counting. I'd got to five when Sebastiano's mum launched her teatime 'Some Of Us Have To Work. Will You Please Keep The Noise Down' routine.

No wonder Seb lived in the bushes.

'Sardines or Heinz tomato soup,' Pa said sadly as he got up from the cupboard. 'With bread,' he said, pushing up the bread bin lid. 'Or, rather, not.'

I don't know why he was so huffy. Bread or no bread, what difference did it make? Seemed Pa, the more he ate the skinnier he got. Must have a tape worm up his bum fat as an eel.

'Sardines or soup or both,' Pa told the cracked tile on the floor.

'I'm full from lunch,' Mo said, her voice as flat as ironing, her Irish ups and downs pressed out.

She glared at that wild Picasso picture, the scary one. He'd got a mad-eyed horse in there, gave it a dagger for a tongue.

'You had no lunch,' said Pa to the sardine can.

What was it about Daniel missing meant we couldn't look at each other any more?

'Ah, well,' Mo said, still staring at the picture.

If I was her I'd get my eyes off that. There was a woman in it, screaming, hanging from one arm a baby, dead, most likely.

'And he can't live on Cheerios,' Pa told the radio behind my head.

'He seems thriving to me,' Mo said, quietly.

I lined my fingers up, flat on the table, made the *Star Trek* sign all to myself.

No Pasaran, that's what Grampy used to say. We're just not having it. I'd look at Mo, right into her face and say, go on, Mo, how about the soup or something.

I clenched my fists for luck and got into position, breathed in deep, and looked.

And found a cold, hard glare that said, 'You didn't check, did you? You little shit. You didn't check my darling Dan was on the coach.'

'Howzat!' Cal screamed.

I couldn't take another second of it. Piggy at fat camp, Pete in Goa, me trapped inside with Mo and Pa and Daniel gone and the itch-itch-itching for something to do.

I rummaged in the downstairs loo for Geoffrey's cricket bat. It was splintery and old, but it was mine. Not even all the big guys had a cricket bat.

'Finish up your Cheerios,' Pa told my back.

'I'm playing cricket with the guys,' I said. It sounded ordinary enough that I might actually dare to do it.

Pa said, 'If Callum asks you back, come in and tell us first.' Then, 'Look after –' and took a break so short you wouldn't notice unless you knew how it was meant to go.

'Look after each other,' he was going to say.

'Look after yourself,' is what he said.

Mo pulled her dressing gown around her and went off up the stairs. Pa swung round, said, 'Mo, where the – I've got the sardines open, ready. Shit!'

He must have dripped sardine slime on his self. I didn't look.

Before their row could start I shut the door behind me and waited in the porch that me and Dan pretended was the air-lock of our battleship. You can't leave both doors open or the ship gets trashed by weather and the sea. Not to mention chemical, biological and nuclear attack. This time it felt like all the badness was on the inside. If I could I'd leave it trapped in there forever and make a new life, on the outside, like a normal person.

If they'd let me.

Biffo said, 'come on, Kid. You can do it! How scary can they be?'

I stepped out, closed the door, took two long breaths – in, out, in, out – and turned to face the square.

Geoffrey's cat coughed up a fur-ball, gave me a one-eyed, who-do-you-think-you-are stare. I wasn't going to let that bother me. Shy Geoffrey leaned on his trowel, looked up, gave me a crooked smile and mumbled something like Hello. My Hello back got mangled just like Geoffrey's.

I opened the gate and strolled across the grass, headed for the barbecue bricks that was our wicket. Swung my cricket bat, nice and casual, like I'd had it all my life. The hot air made me thirsty. I was feeling kind of shaky. I should have had a drink and then a wee.

A lady with fat arms glanced up from her rug and nudged her friend and said something, most likely nasty. I felt like any second all the square would turn at once and spear me with their eyes and say, 'So, you're the boy.'

They didn't, though.

I walked.

Mrs Gomez threw a wobbly because someone, and They'd Better Not Think She Didn't Know Who They Were, had left the hosepipe running. Ben and Sebastiano wrestled in the bushes. Sunbathers lolled about, their clothes on now, thumbing through magazines and books and stuff. Speccy Bernstein played his Gameboy. And over by the wicket Milly's dad got all steamed up at Callum while Milly yelled her happy head off.

In other words, life carried on out there exactly as before. Seemed nobody but Geoffrey, his cat and Mrs Fat-arms even saw me and maybe she was just admiring my cricket bat after all. I could pick my way around the square people like an invisible man or like a ghost.

I kept on walking.

The gay guys served out their sushi takeaway. Cal's mum, in her deck chair, all alone, tipped up her bottle, got the last few drops of wine into her glass. Cal's baby sister, Little P, trotted round and offered sweets to all the kids.

I made it to the wicket! I actually made it!

Straightaway I wished I hadn't. Milly's dad wagged his finger angrily at Cal who gripped in two tight hands a, oh, no, a black aluminium baseball bat. I tried to get my cricket bat behind me. You can imagine what a twat I felt.

'Cal,' I said.

'Is this entirely safe?' said Milly's dad, who's always asking questions when he already knows the answers on account of he's a teacher.

Milly smiled and swung her legs under her stool and yelled, 'I'm eatin my dinner outside, today!'

Milly's mum said in her funny foreign accent, 'I don't sink ze holl skvare needs to know.'

Cal squinted up at Milly's dad and said, 'It's very safe, actually. It's the wooden ones that break on you.'

'I'm havin eggs,' yelled Milly.

The other end of the square, the fielders, Jamal and Hairy Zac, didn't notice me. They kicked the grass and made the tosser sign at Milly's dad.

'It's not the bat that concerns me,' he banged on. 'It's the enormous velocity of the ball coming back at a multiple of the speed with which it's thrown.' He scratched his burnt bald patch. I'm glad that hurt.

Cal gave Milly's dad his vacant look.

'Cal,' I said.

'It's a simple matter of basic physics.'

Cal looked like he'd never heard of that.

'I'm havin eggs,' yelled Milly.

'Get on and av zem zen,' said Milly's mum.

Jamal and Hairy Zac mobbed Little P, took some of her lollies and muzzed her curly hair. Sunbathers rustled their pages and rolled over like they'd had just about enough of Milly's parents. Cal's mum cursed her corkscrew and started opening another bottle.

'I think you'll find that aluminium increases the velocity of the ball enormously,' said Milly's dad.

Cal scratched his balls.

Pop, said the cork. Little P strolled over, smiled at Milly, held out her little bag.

Milly's mum said, 'No sank you, dalling, Milly's eating now her ex.'

The smile on Little P turned soft and wobbly.

Milly said, 'Lolly first. Eggs later,' took one, gave Little P a happy grin.

'I don't expect she'll vont her ex now. Tell your muzza sank you very much indeed,' Milly's mum told Little P in a hard, dry voice that meant the opposite of what it said.

Across the square Cal's mum lit up a fag.

'Let me have a look at that,' said Milly's dad, reaching out for Callum's bat.

'Oh, no you don't,' Cal said and snatched it clean away.

'Cal,' I said.

'I need a pee!' cried Milly.

'You should play in the park, big boys like you.'

'I'll make a pee pee in the bushes,' Milly said.

Milly's dad swept round and snapped, 'You'll do it in the toilet, in the house, my girl.'

'Cal.'

He made as if he hadn't heard me and slipped off towards the fielders. I stood there like a spastic with my cricket bat.

Milly pulled her knickers down and said, 'I want to do it in the bushes.'

'Melissa, dogs and cats go in the bushes,' said Milly's dad.

Milly's mum said, 'Are you a dock?' and pulled her knickers up again.

Cal and the big guys gathered up their stuff and headed off for Cal's to play his drum machine or something cool, I bet.

'I'm havin the accident,' yelled Milly.

'I don't believe you are,' said Milly's dad.

The gay guys got the giggles.

'I'm havin it! I'm havin it!' yelled Milly.

'Right Now My Girl Into The House,' said Milly's dad. He picked her up just like she was a rugby ball and ran her down the square like he was running for a try, weaving round the rumpled blankets of the sunbathers that rippled now with giggles spreading out from round the gay guys. Round the bushes, through their gate, and . . .

'I'm havin it!' cried Milly.

Touchdown!

'Damn my trousers!'

Milly sobbed, 'I want my lolly, now,' and then their door slammed shut.

Milly's mother glared across the sunbathers to Cal and Little P's mum: 'You see, ze trabble now viz zvates.'

Cal's mum took one long drag on her cigarette, blew a smoke ring, then another one that plipped right through the first. She watched them rise and break, then lifted up her glass and did a bleary Cheers to Milly's mum while all the time the one-eyed cat was sicking up on Milly's eggs.

Daniel gone, and people still got all wound up at Callum's bat and growing-food and pissing in the bushes. I hated them. I wanted to be one of them.

'Harry,' said a little voice. I looked around me. No-one there.

'Harry,' said the voice. Someone tugged my trousers. I looked down. Little P.

'Yo-yi?' she said. I put my hand into her bag but it was empty.

I took a lolly, anyway, an invisible lolly. She seemed glad. I gave the lolly a ghost of a lick and felt in her bag for another.

'Here's one for you,' I said and muzzed her curly hair, then I strolled back, nice and casual, an invisible man with an invisible lolly. I swung my stupid splintery cricket bat and wondered how I'd get across the empty grave that stretched out wide and cold and lonely between me and my bed-time.

'Hi, Harry.' Speccy Bernstein by our gate.

'Hi, Josh,' I said and kept on moving. Speccy bloody Bernstein. I wasn't completely desperate.

8

'Yabba-Dabba-Doo!' Terry yelled as he launched himself off the springboard and flew. High above me he stopped – impossible, I know. Then he swooped and landed so close I felt his breath on my face.

'Wicked!' I said.

Terry dusted himself down, growled, 'Yours weren't all bad.'

'Nowhere near as high as yours, Terry.'

I must not sound too keen. I mustn't blow my big chance to be Terry's mate.

I said, 'My go!'

He said, 'We've finished that.'

I didn't mind Terry giving out the orders on account of I didn't have any ideas of my own. Terry filled your head, kept your mind off the badness. A holiday from Daniel missing, from Mo and Pa, the row and the itching for something to do.

He yawned, pulled back his arms in a long, lazy stretch. He had bumps in them, muscles, they'd be hard if you touched them.

'I'm gonna give you a present, Harry, a reward.'

He stood so close it hurt my neck to look up at him. I

expect it was so the gardener couldn't snoop on our manoeuvres. Enemy spies come in all sorts of disguises. Terry
reached into his battle fatigues, pulled out his fist, unfolded
it one finger at a time.

'Look.'

He turned the prize in the air. It caught the sun. I was
dazzled. My mouth fell open. I tried to control it, felt my
face twist.

'I said look, not touch.' His cold, blue eyes in his hot,
freckly face, there was something weird about them. Like if
you got your finger in and touched one, it would stick to
you like prickly ice and hurt you.

'Pay attention, Pickles. Commando weapon. Top secret.'
He snapped it open at scissors, the pointy ends so close to
my eyes they were blurred.

Some kids might be frightened. Not me. I was a commando at a top secret SAS training centre, Terry, the world-
famous weapons expert taking me through the drill.

Snap. Tweezers. 'In case of scorpion bites.' They looked
just the kind Mo used to weed her eyebrows.

Snap. Snap. A bottle opener, screwdrivers – for bomb dis-
posal, Terry said.

Peter would puke if he knew about me and Terry, all
this top-secret stuff. Tough luck on him. He should have
thought of that before the three-legged race.

Snap. Chisel. *Snap.* Dagger.

That's what got me excited, the dagger.

'Fantastic. Thanks a million, Terry.'

'Not so quick, Pickles. Forfeit first.'

* * *

Terry was one of those super-lucky orphans you read about. He lived in a white mansion by Holland Park with a gigantic garden that was virtually Terry's own on account of his neighbours being away all summer on their Caribbean islands. He had a servant, called Consuela, who had to wear a uniform and do everything he told her. His parents weren't dead exactly, just so rich they were never at home, plus his dad had to go on these SAS special manoeuvres that were so completely top secret they had to keep Terry's mum in the dark.

'Put this on,' he said.

A silky balaclava. Probably used in a siege or something. I pulled it over my head. Through the hole I watched the gardener sharpening a blade. You could hear the scraping on the breeze that brought the smell of just cut grass. Terry twisted the balaclava round, shoved something scratchy over the top, a woolly hat, it felt like. I couldn't see a thing and I couldn't hear much neither.

He spun me round and whispered, 'Find me.' Then, without any noise, he was gone.

It's hard to consider your strategic strengths like commandos are supposed to with the sun beating down on your woolly-hatted head.

I shouted, 'I know exactly where you are!'

Which is what I would have yelled at Daniel.

'Oh, no you don't,' he'd sing back at me. Then I'd go get him. Grown-ups said Daniel was a bright spark. What did they know?

It didn't work on Terry, obviously, and I felt the idiot, my words floating out there. Was that how Dan Dan felt, now, shouting out and no-one coming?

'Harry!' snapped Terry from right next to me. I nearly wet myself.

'One more thing about the SAS info. One single word to anyone, I have to kill you.'

Then he really legged it, far, far away. I listened for the gardener, heard traffic grumbling and a plane high above, packed with happy people on their holidays, most likely, going somewhere like Barbados. My face itched with sweat. My mouth was dry. I felt lonelier than when I played all alone, and so completely crap, I mean, it was supposed to be fun and this was no fun at all.

'Kid, you don't have to go along with this,' said Biffo. 'Don't seem right to me unless the guy's prepared to take turns.'

'But he's the leader.'

'And what are you, Kid?'

'I'm –'

'You do everything a person tells you where I come from there's a word for what you are.'

'You're not helping.'

'I'll help you, Kid. OK. That's what you want, run.'

'You must be crazy!'

'I may be crazy but I'm not blind. Run. I'll be your eyes. Have faith.'

I thought of the weapon and being Terry's mate and I ran. The fastest blind boy runner in the world!

'Veer left,' said Biffo. A twig thwacked my face.

'I said left, you klutz! Left! Now, slow down. Take it easy. Wooo. Use your nose. Think with your nose.'

I breathed in and really thought about it. I smelt sweaty hat, the dark solid scent of earth rising up on the heat. Eucalyptus oil Mo rubbed on Dan when he was wheezy. Then, somewhere over there, just over there, I was sure of it, the smell, I don't know what you call it, the smell of boy. Terry's own special tanginess arrived next.

'Gotcha!' I said.

Out of him came a heat so fierce I thought he'd punch me in the face.

But he didn't.

'Harry, you mad bastard. Sprinting at trees like that. You could have brained yourself. You're really wild, you know?'

He pulled off the blindfolds. Colours rushed in on me. The sun had scorched the grass brown, turned the earth dry and dusty, how Africa looked. Terry's freckles seemed to glow in the heat. Terry in his orangey kingdom. A tiger in the jungle. My mate.

He said, 'Some guys talk like they're wild and some guys really are. Know what I mean?'

Peter was the talking wild kind of guy.

Terry took my face in both his hands and rubbed his nose against mine, not just the tips, both our whole faces seemed to be involved. I tasted salt and oranges. I didn't pull away.

I half-wanted the gardener to see us, see that I was Terry's mate and someone special too, like Terry. And if the gardener was an enemy spy, so what? He could write all about me in secret code to the enemy top brass, I wouldn't mind.

Out loud I said, 'About that weapon, Terry.'

He laughed. 'That wasn't the forfeit! Nah. The forfeit

97

happens later. But you won't know til after. How does that sound?'

'Wicked,' I said.

'Don't sound good to me,' said Biffo. 'Looks like this joker's got you just exactly where he wants you.'

9

Me, Otis and Joan, we're groaning and pushing this huge cake on wheels. Jesus, it's heavy.

Mo's all giggles, eyes closed, 'What's going on?'

Pa hits the lights. 'Just you wait, hun.'

Otis fires up the candles, millions of them, seems like.

Joan whispers, 'Open your eyes.'

Out of the darkness Mo's eyes flash, her face glows with the flames and excitement, she takes a deep breath, we all hold ours and –

'Da Daaah!'

Dan shoots out of the cake on a pneumatic platform. He's got his Superman jimjams on, pants over the top.

'Da Daaah!'

What a triffic birthday surprise!

Light bounces off Mo's eyes and her earrings and her slinky silver dress. We all float up to the ceiling and bounce about laughing – 'Hip Hip Hooray!' – that's how happy we are.

'Not this time.'

'But, Pa.'

'No.'

'A card at least.'

'Harry, look at me.' Suds dripped off the fingers of his yellow rubber gloves. 'No card. No present. No whining.'

This time it's the world's biggest chocolate fudge brownie – on rails. Otis sprays the candles with a flame-thrower. I'm just getting to the bit where Daniel springs out when in real life Mo sleep-walked in, a tea-stain on her dressing gown, eyes blank, hair greasy. Mo, thirty-nine today. Looking every minute of it.

She said, 'I thought I might,' left it hanging, shuffled off again.

Mo's birthday. Sunshine. Lots of reasons to be cheerful. Not at our house. Oh, no. Life dragged on.

Weheyhey! Look, no hands! Me on my Trek Mountain Lion Bike, swerving round tourists down Elgin Avenue. Don't you love that ripping sound of tyre on hot road?

Mister Boombastic, blasting out of a sound system someone's dusting off from last year. Giggly kids, all excited about the Carnival that's coming, half dressed up as peacocks, bumble-bees, all sorts, sparkle like marbles in the sun.

Mo would get her present, whether she liked it or not. No matter how bad things are you have to celebrate stuff, else you might as well give up and die.

No Pasaran.

Thirty-nine lengths I'd swim for her, all-time record for me. Might not even tell her. It's the thought that counts.

'That's the ticket,' said Biffo. 'That's the spirit, Kid. I'm prouda ya.'

I felt so good I said, 'Hey, Biffo, why don't you have a break? Go on, mate, have a holiday.'

Queuing for tickets you could hear drums pounding, a band out there doing some practice for the Carnival.

'Certainly hot, I'll give you that,' said a man behind me.

'No sign of rain, please God,' said a lady.

People talked like that, getting cosy with strangers coming up to the Carnival. It was our Carnival. All of us. We actually lived there, and all those people who spilled out of the tube were just visitors.

'It'll be a sizzler, I bet,' I said, not out loud, though.

Nine Carnivals I'd been to. Ten, if you count the one I was in Mo's tummy. Dan said it was him that time. Wasn't, though. You can ask her. Ten Carnivals. The original *Mister Boombastic*, that's me.

'Are you with us, love, are you in the land of the living?'

I certainly was.

'One junior swim, please.'

'Are you here for Happy Dippers, the disabled kiddies?'

Obviously I wasn't.

'If you're not a Happy Dipper, there's fifteen minutes left, love. Do you still want to pay for the session?'

Fifteen minutes, fifteen lengths. Tops.

I gave her the money.

'You'll be needing a pound for the lockers, love.'

'I've got my pound,' I said, loudly, in case people thought I was a Dippy Hopper who looks all right but is funny in the head.

The gents smelt stronger than the ladies. Felt different too. More grown-up. Less chat. Bit scary. Men trying not to be watching each other. In the ladies, with Mo, didn't hardly notice other people about, what with Mo at us to hurry up and get on, and me and Dan flicking each other's bums with our towels.

Leapt right over the footbath, the drum beat getting louder. Ten minutes left, said the big clock. Ten lengths, tops. Best speed up.

'No ranning at ze boolside!'

That big German lifeguard. I'd show him. There's no rule against goose-stepping, Herr Prick.

'You! Offa hare! Haff you shard?'

'Course I have.' Actually, I'd rubbed spit in my hair.

'Shar again, please.'

Brilliant showers. Freezing cold. Scorching hot.

The big clock says seven minutes. Seven lengths. Never mind, it's the thought that counts. No running this time. No goose-stepping neither.

Got in.

Nice feeling isn't it, hot pee on cold legs? Didn't catch me this time, did you, Herr Prick?

Thought of Mo and pushed off into the cool blue light. Torpedo Kid, that's me, shooting over where the floor falls into the deep, the drums, drumming me on. Bubbles tickled my ears. Felt a safe, locked-in feeling.

Those drums, every year, drummed Mo's birthday and the Carnival in. And the first off-beat beats of kids rehearsing in the Methodist hall sent me and Pa and Daniel off down Oxford Street to get Mo's presents and our new term equipment, eat bacon sandwiches, stare down on tiny shoppers from the fifth floor of John Lewis.

Once, after Mo's birthday supper, the drums woke me up. Smelt burning. Ran downstairs, ready to rush the whole entire family into the safety of the night and the fire crews' blues and twos. (That's blue lights and two-tone sirens if you've not got a fireman in your family.) Found Mo and Joan snuggled up on the sofa, red-eyed and cosy. Red wine and chocolate. Funny-looking cigarette. Just the one — they took turns.

'No, Harry, darling, no gorgeous, no, there isn't a fire.'

'Have a cuddle H. In the middle. Mmmm. Lovely boy.'

Voices thin and croaky. They couldn't stop giggling.

Made it! All the way to the murals of sea snakes and mermaids. A whole length underwater. Personal world record best. For Mo. Surfaced, gasping, to the thunder of drums.

The next bit just happened. Crossed my arms over my chest, tucked my elbows in, chin down, let myself

drop,

drop,

drop

to the bottom.

Stood there. Didn't know you could do that. Yellow waves of light danced across the floor. Liked the pressure on my ears. Closed my eyes. A trapdoor opened. Sucked me down, down. How long would drowning take? Did it hurt?

Last time Pa took us swimming, Dan stood on the edge, checked for Herr Flick.

'Geronimo!' Dive-bombed me.

Pa, no idea it wasn't allowed:

'Well done, Daniel! You're really getting the hang of this.'

Helped him up again. Dan whipped off his inflatables.

'Geronimo!'

Splash!

Pa, sorting out the armbands. Things always went missing when he was in charge.

'Pa, he hasn't surfaced yet.'

'Course you can, honey.'

'Pa, Pa, Pa. He's still down there.'

'Wha—!'

Pa yanked him off the bottom. Dan's sick hit Pa's chest. Fear hit Pa's face.

That's how fast Pa could move, before, you know. Faster than fear.

Drowning not as easy as you think, most likely. Herr Prick would spoil it, save me, do the kiss of life in front of everybody. I flapped my hands. Rose towards light. Sped up, shot out, really like a torpedo, gulping for air.

A pair of giant clogs, big face loomed over me.

'I vont zay it again. Iz Happy Dippuz. Clare ze bool.'

'But the clock. The big clock. It's ages yet.'

He tapped his watch, the sort that divers use ten thousand metres under water.

'Ziz ere. Ziz iz ze tamepiss zat carnts.'

Nazi.

In the changing rooms Dippy Hoppers clanked about. I got dressed, pretended not to look, had a sneaky-peeky. Least I had all my bits.

Jumped between the sliding doors. Blasted by sunlight and *Mister Boombastic* bang on time just for me.

How about no hands all the way home to make up for the lengths? A nail-biting, death-dicing first. For Mo. It's the thought that counts, isn't it?

Must have stood at the bike rack a good while dreaming. Loads of bikes. Not one of them mine. Tru-Pro-Lok still there. Took a while for the penny to drop. Moron. Idiot. Dickhead. Must have locked it straight to the bar, left the bike out. Fuck-fuck-fuck-fuckwit.

Wouldn't you think that if you lost your little brother and your mountain bike all in one summer, you wouldn't give a monkey's about your bike?

Well, you'd be wrong about that.

I hid my Tru-Pro-Lok with my other precious stuff under Daniel's bed and got ready to tell Mo about my lengths. I stood tall and loose, closed my eyes, breathed all the way in, then all the way out. All the way, how Otis taught me, til my chest was like, this big, and I was three centimetres taller.

In my head I said, 'I am strong. I am ready.' And I was. I really was. I would have done it, only down in the kitchen they were rowing again.

10

If I could just stay still, absolutely still, grip the bark with the backs of my legs and my fingernails. Terry-n-Harry, Harry-n-Terry. Sounded good whichever way you said it. I tried to focus on that, keep myself from thinking about the drop and the ground that would jump right up to kill me if I dared even to look.

'Does this kid know about your problem?'

'Jesus, Biffo. Stay away, all right?'

Just thinking made me want to puke. We must have been like fifty metres up the tree.

'OK, Kid, you're the boss.'

He said it like I wasn't the boss, but I couldn't be thinking about that, because Terry was standing, balanced on the branch, pulling on a rope that led through a hole, down, down, actually inside the tree. Out popped an army rucksack.

Terry squatted down, nice and casual, like he'd never heard of quadrapleejix, and slid two tin-foil packages from the rucksack, carefully, like they were Semtex.

If I could just stay —

'Catch!'

Weheyhey!

I caught it, actually caught it, didn't fall and snap my neck.

I unwrapped the foil, one-handed, so I could keep one hand on the tree, taking care in case of booby-traps.

Sandwiches.

'Sheep droppings,' he said.

'You're kidding.' He wouldn't be. Terry never saw the point of that.

'Slugs, berries, worms, you name it. A commando'll eat anything to survive.'

'Kid, some things you just don't do, for dignity's sake.' Bloody Biffo. Sounded like Mo talking. 'Don't you think eating shit might just be one of them?' Smart Arse. Terry bit into his sandwich, didn't say what he was having.

Terry was completely totally brilliant. He had black in-line skates, a whole room for Scalextric, his own personal tennis coach, a cricket coach and on top of all them he had his very own therapist, which is a person that has to listen to your troubles for a whole entire hour every week without interrupting even once. His mum was really important, bought bits of companies or something, then, like, closed them down. I don't know how that works exactly but it's wicked.

'Wassup, Harry? Lost your appetite?'

Terry watched, waited for me to take a bite. I cast about for something to distract him, but looking down there made Cheerios and milk and acid slosh horribly in my belly. I looked into his cold blue eyes for inspiration but found, it's funny, this, found absolutely nothing there.

Off the top of my head, I said,

'How come you're at Mandela's, Tel?'

He said, 'You mean instead of public school?'

'Well, yes.' No-one at our school was rich like Terry.

'Used to be. Got sent to Mandela's for a punishment.'

'Why'd they want to punish you for?' I peeled back the roof of my sandwich.

'Got expelled.'

'Expelled! What for?' Little curranty things. Sultanas, maybe. I didn't like to risk it, though.

'Hated it.'

'But, why?'

'The usual.'

'What, bullying?'

'They never proved it, Harry.' You could see from his face he didn't mean to say that. He checked the compass on a chain around his neck and glared out across the garden. 'It's hard to explain boarding school to someone who's never done it. Imagine living with your teachers.'

A camping trip with Miss Bliss, just the two of us, was all I came up with.

'They expelled you just for hating it?'

Terry pulled binoculars from the bag. I prepared to jettison that stuff from my sandwich.

'Nah. I said I hated it. Dad said it was character building. I had to do something.'

'Like what?'

'Oh, you know.' The binoculars seemed to shake in Terry's hands. His face went red and kind of sweaty. I wondered if he'd wet the bed. 'Going down the shops without permission. Look, Harry. Can we change the record?'

'I'm interested is all. D'you do anything else?'

'Loads of cool stuff, you know.' He put the binoculars to

his eyes and scanned the garden. I flicked those things — *ping, ping, ping* — and watched them fall. It was an awful long way down. He said, 'Bit of thieving. Arson.'

'My Uncle Otis —'

'Books at first,' said Terry. 'Really winds them up. Still didn't throw me out. Had to think bigger.'

I saw whole shelves of books on fire.

'I torched the shed.'

I dropped my sandwich.

'What?'

'The shed, you know, where they keep the roller for the cricket pitch. Got a fuel tank. Big bang.'

Best not mention Otis, then.

'That got things moving. Mmm.' Terry fixed his binoculars on one particular point. 'It looked rather like that one.'

The neat wooden shed, a Hansel and Gretel cottage with a water barrel to one side, a bench out front. Imagine! Burning that!

And here was me, Harry Pickles, up a tree with a real life arsonist who'd actually been expelled!

My heart pounded low in my belly. The sun had that reddish glow it gets before the grown-ups call you in. It caught Terry's ginger hair, seemed like he'd set his head alight.

He frowned into the binoculars.

'Got him. Deep in enemy territory. Guy acting suspiciously. Hell's teeth. You know who that is, Harry?'

I saw the gardener, in front of the shed, pottering about.

'It's him, isn't it, Harry? Tell me, it's him.'

'It's him, all right.' I had absolutely no idea what Terry was on about.

'I expect he does his driving on his days off from here.

The police asked all those questions about him, didn't they? Dirty bastard.'

The bus driver?

'Just think, Harry, what he did. Dirty bastard. Dirty bloody bastard.'

'But, Terry, the thing is –'

'I say we do him.'

'What?'

'You're not turning chicken on me, are you?'

'No, but –'

'No buts, Harry. No buts in soldiering. Dirty bastard.'

I watched the man wipe some sort of blade with a rag, put the blade on the bench, shake the rag, fold it, set it down. Something in the way he went about his work, one thing at a time.

'Think what he did, Harry.'

Please, no. I squeezed my eyes tight shut.

'Out here, like he's got away with it. I shouldn't stand for it, Harry.'

That man, tidying things away like he had something to hide, Terry going on at me. The hot sun, my dry mouth, the terrible drop. Those pictures crackling into life. Real life and games swirled about and bashed against each other.

'Now now now waid a seggund. Hold arn here, Kiddo. I –'

'Biffo, just stay out of it.'

'Seems to me, I don't like to prejudge a person, but seems to me you should go easy, this guy has ishoos.'

'Ishoos?' Cal's mum had some of them.

'Ishoos, Kid. I don't like to –'

'Stay out of it. It's not for real. None of your business.'

'Sounds kinda real to me and –'

'That's –'

'And, Kid, if you will let me finish, Kid, you *are* my business.'

Terry took the binoculars from his eyes and wiped his face. If I didn't know him better I'd say that he was crying. He coughed and kind of pulled himself together and said, 'We've got some investigating to do.'

Of course, that was the thing. Investigate first.

11

Tap tap tap tappety tap. Tap tap tap tappety tap. Tappety tap tap.

Pa and his new best friend Otis, out on the patio, skipping together like a big pair of poofs. Biffo going on at me.

'Kid, don't you think the police should know?'

'It's all top secret.'

'Kid, the lady said anything comes up, anything at all.'

'Who, Wendy?'

'Sure. Wendy. She said –'

Tap tap tap tappety tap. Tap tap tap tappety tap. Tappety tap tap.

It got on your nerves after a bit.

'Wendy? What use is Wendy? Wendy's crap.'

David Beckham's crap, as well. I don't mean in real life. No, in real life he's my absolute all-time hero. I mean in World Cup Soccer, the computer game. He let me down badly. Pickles Drops Beckham! Why not?

Tap tap tap tappety tap.

Trouble was, Michael Owen wasn't up to it either. In fact the whole squad was useless. So I bollocked them and I walked. Found a team that deserved my style of management.

Tappety. Tappety. Tappety. Tappety.

Brazil Welcomes Pickles!

That's more like it. Decided to take challenges from the little countries, Switzerland, Luxembourg, give my boys a chance to bang some goals in.

Oh.

Maybe it was the underdog factor, all that pressure on Brazil to perform.

Tap tap tap tappety tap.

Or the distractions.

I clicked QUIT.

Are you sure you want to quit?

Too right I'm sure.

Tap tap tap tappety tap. Tap tap tap tappety tap.

Jesus!

'Kid, a promise don't count if it aint honourable.'

'Not you again.'

'Talk it over with your uncle. In confidence.'

Tappety, tappety, tappety.

'Confidence?'

'Like in a confessional.'

'Confessional?'

Tap tap tap tappety tap. Tap tap tap tappety tap.

'For Christ's sake.'

The tapping stopped. I closed my eyes.

'Kid, believe me, you need to talk it over.'

'Leave it, will you? I need a bit of peace.'

'You're the boss.'
Quiet. Peace and Quiet.
Yeah, that's better.
Bam Bam Bam Bam Bameddy Bam.
Jesus!
'Kid, you —'
'All right. All right. I'll talk to him.'

I scooted down the stairs, out to the patio, watched Otis corner Pa.

'Crowdin you, baby, crowdin you.' Otis held up the right pad.

Pa struck: *flump.* Landed like jelly.

'Sorry, sorry,' Pa breathed.

Otis, pads up again. Faster this time. Left. Right. Left.

I made a little cough.

Otis to Pa, 'Here for a lark?'

Pa touched his glove against his nose, sniffed. His face shone with sweat.

I said, 'Er, excuse me.'

Pads up. Pa punched, moved forwards.

Otis backed off a bit.

'Better, baby, better. Don't want me crowdin you. Now. Give it some muscle.'

Pa hurled punches.

Flump, flump. Flump, flump.

'Freeze!' said Otis.

I froze. So did Pa.

'Excuse me, please, Otis.'

'Not now, Harry. Your hands, Dom! Look at yourself.

Holdin your shorts up.'

Otis tapped him on the bum.

'Hands up, up. Protecting here's what you want.'

Slapped him in the face.

Pa got his hands up, stood like a real boxer, kind of.

Otis looked at him like he'd never seen anything so pathetic.

'Thirty seconds.'

Pa's hands dropped like he had rocks in his gloves.

'Hey, Otis, when you've got a minute?'

Otis turned his eyes on me.

'This here's the gym, Harry. Not the garden, when we're sparring. Certain rules apply. You can watch but you can't talk. Right?'

What? What? What? Whose garden was it, anyway?

I said, 'You think it's a horrid sport, don't you, Pa?'

'Please, Harry, not now.'

'For blockheads and brutes, you said.'

I could tell Otis what Pa really thought of him. That'd show them. Decided not to, this time. Left them to it, hoped they'd break each other's noses.

12

I soft-footed it to Mo and Pa's room to find the last stuff I needed for my mission kit, listening out in case something happened and they needed my help. They were having that row again, tighter and sharper as if, like everyone else before the Carnival, they were drumming up towards the big day.

'Only a suggestion,' Pa said softly. 'Not an attack.'

'I don't need your suggestions, Doctor, thank you, and I don't need your professional advice. Let's say I start tomorrow. Let's say I do.'

Mo, beginning quietly, like the alarm clock that gets louder and louder til it splits bones in your head.

'You! You! You just walk back into your surgery. What do I do? What the fuck do I do? A welcome back to Mo Tully in the *Guardian*? A successor column to Me and My Boys? Ooops, Honey I Lost The Kid?'

I heard the *Archers* music coming through the wall. Shy Geoffrey turning up his radio to be polite, most likely.

I searched through Mo's drawers for stockings me and Terry needed to pull over our faces, like bank robbers, so we wouldn't get picked out in an identity parade.

Pa, quietly, 'I'm not saying you have to do the column.'

Me and Terry had got together a criminal profile like real detectives and committed it to memory so it couldn't be used for evidence if we got caught. The gardener was called Dennis, which might be his first name, his surname or an alias. He rode a bike, but once Terry spotted him getting off the number 53 bus in a suspicious manner. He did things carefully, but he left half a canister of petrol outside the shed one day and didn't notice when it was gone.

Mo snarled, 'Mo's latest: Me and My Loss.'

'I'm not saying you *have* to do anything.'

'If you thought Julie Burchill was a sad old cow, try Me and My Marriage, the latest column from . . .'

Me and Terry had collected, among other things, the secret weapon, the skipping rope, two Bic lighters, a potato peeler in case we had to do some torturing, and the petrol. I was going to borrow Pa's razor, but it cut me when I opened it. We were still working on our fire-making experiments.

'Mo, stop it. I am not the enemy. All I said was it might help if you took on something that would lend a little structure, add a little . . .'

No stockings, just pants, more pants and buried at the bottom some lacy stuff looked like it'd scratch her wotnot.

'Sometimes work helps.'

These days Mo couldn't speak, hardly. Writing was more difficult. Didn't Pa know? Seemed someone had taken half his brain away. Should he be going to the surgery? What was he doing to those patients of his?

'Good morning, Dr Pickles, I've split my head open. Smashed like a watermelon, it is.'

'Have an aspirin. Next!'

'Oooh these ingrowing toenails are troubling me something rotten, Doc.'

'Nurse! Pass me the chainsaw. We'll soon have this sorted.'

Zzzzzz.

'Argggh!'

Kerplonk!

'Me leg!'

'Next! Good morning, Mrs Thingybob, what can I do for you?'

'It's my son, Dr Pickles, he has this terrible hacking cough.'

'Least you've got a son, Mrs T. Should think yourself lucky. Next!'

We'd been working on rubbing sticks together, in case we ran out of lighter fuel. You have to be ready for anything. I fluffed the pants about. You wouldn't know I'd been there.

'You know what I need!' I hoped that wasn't my hippo mug Mo was smashing.

'Please, not that again.' Pa sounded in pain.

'Please Not That Again,' Mo, spitting. 'Why can't we discuss it? Why can't you –'

A drum band drew up. Something loud, fast, excited, all I could hear. I found tangles of tights, what did she want with them all? Tights might be as good, come to think of it. You didn't have to use the extra leg. The drums moved on.

'You know it wouldn't be –'

'Go on, Dom, say it.' Calmer now. Not in a nice way. 'You can't even say his name.'

Rubbing sticks together doesn't work, by the way. A magnifying lens, the sun and paper's a much better bet. I got out the commando weapon, snapped it open at the scissors. You had to stretch the tights out across your hand to cut it cleanly. Nice sound it made.

'We need time.' Pa, gently.

'I'm thirty-nine!'

'But it's grotesque, Mo!'

He maybe tried to cuddle her or something, cos what happened next was she spat, 'Get your fucking hands off me then!'

There was a kind of wrestle, then Pa said, low and slow, 'I know it's what you say you want, now, in the midst of this horror.'

'Not what I *want*, Dom. What I *need*, what *we* need, the one thing that might help pull us through.'

Something cold about her. I mean, like, made you shiver.

I pulled one leg down over my head.

'There's Harry, Mo. We've got to pull through. For Harry.'

In the mirror, Harry Pickles with a squashed nose and funny shaped eyes. You'd have no trouble telling it was me.

'Harry?' Mo, cold, cold.

You had to be patient, making fire the lens way. For ages the paper only darkened and if a cloud hid the sun, you had to wait. Then, when you'd given up hope:

'Harry?' she said. 'Harry's Not Enough.'

Pfffff! An explosion of fire.

'I said five minutes, Sebastiano.'

Would she ever shut up? I needed my sleep. D-Day might be any minute.

I went to close the window, pulled up the blind, hadn't

noticed before that bald patch on the top of his head. Pa, tap tap tapping on the patio, arms stretched like Jesus on the cross. Pete's Jesus hanging over his kitchen table only Pete's Jesus had blood spurting out and his head lolling down and was already dead. You could hardly see the leather moving Pa flicked it so fast. He skipped faster and faster, the boxer's way, right, right, left, left. His T-shirt stuck to his back. Hottest summer for years, they said.

'Sebastiano. I'm not asking you again.'

She would, though.

I lay down on my bed, pulled the duvet up, too hot for that, but I needed the weight of it, closed my eyes, held my willy. Now and then tube trains zipped by above Barlby Road where Dan used to run out and dance, crazy idiot, trying to get a laugh from the commuters.

To keep from dreaming I listened for the trains. I heard Pa's tap-tap-tapping, Mo's low moaning, the drums and the reggae, jungle-music in the distance.

'Sebastiano! Now!'

Seemed every single thing in my world except me had a beat to it.

Here come the trains.

Yanottinuff, Yanottinuff, Yanottinuff, said the trains.

I held tight to Pa's *tap-tap-tap*.

Blue-grey fog swirled round us. I could tell by the way my ears hurt and the engine strained that we were high up in mountains. Which would account for the teeth-rattling cold. We were coming to a junction. Trees, shaped like daggers, flicked by. I tried to read the sign, get some idea where we were headed. A word so long it might be Welsh. Loo-something. Loo-something. Fuzzy letters blended.

'Lookaftereachother,' it said.

Dan, small, pale, hunched, like the time he wheezed so hard he ended up in Casualty.

I should be doing something, I didn't know what, my thoughts froze in thinking, doing something, maybe scraping around for a torch or Dan's Ventolin or a knife. I blew on my hands, tucked them inside my jimjam jacket. We needed fleeces, long trousers, anoraks. Socks would have helped. Shame the driver hadn't got us a rug or something instead of that stupid stuff he'd bought. Four rolls of thick white tape people use for painting round windows. Bin bags, black ones. A spade, brand new — never seen one so shiny.

You'd think it couldn't get any colder. Then he spoke.

'Let's see, now. I'd like Mrs Pill, the Doctor's wife.'

'I'm collecting Pills,' snapped Dan.

That was extremely rude for Daniel. If you knew him, you'd understand he was being very rude indeed. Anyone could collect the doctor's family if they had one already. It was completely allowed by the rules.

'Mrs Pill, please,' said the man.

Dan didn't have Mrs Pill, I don't know why the man was on at him. I didn't have her either.

'You can't hide anything from me, Dan Dan.'

He shouldn't be saying Dan Dan. Only me, Mo and Pa were allowed. I would have said so, but the fear and something worse had got its fingernails dug into my voice.

'I'm not asking you, I'm telling you. Mrs Pill, the doctor's wife.'

Dan slid a card from under his thigh. His face was different, he was kind of grown-up in his face. Like he knew something I didn't. Something horrid. But he wasn't even five.

Out of the speakers came that cheery song the driver liked.

'No secrets, Daniel. No secrets from me.'

The one about things getting better.

Dan put the card face down by the man's other cards. That man hadn't managed to collect any grown-ups.

Inside my head, like he was talking only to me, the man's icy voice,

'You know your problem, Harry? You're not enough. You're not enough.'

Dan turned the card.

Mrs Pill, the doctor's wife, she didn't look at all like the others. Dark shiny hair, nearly black eyebrows, blue gleaming eyes, she was easily the best-looking parent in the pack.

13

'It's nice to be out,' said Joan.

Obviously it wasn't.

If you'd just touched down from Mars you could tell that everyone on Clarendon Road was heading for a party.

That goofy white couple, khaki shorts, whistles round their necks.

Sound systems warming up: 'Would you like to rock it with me, bay-bee?'

Moody black girls eyed up moody black boys, the air between them so hot you could strike a match and set the street on fire.

'Would you like to jam it with me, hon-ey?'

Everyone excited, everyone up for it, everyone except us, that is, creeping along in the opposite direction like we had some kind of allergy to fun.

Joan tried to set a pace. Mo's feet went slower and slower. Walking after Grampy's coffin through that muddy grave-yard in the rain felt this way. Funeral time.

'Come and jam it with me, hon-ey.'

For all Joan's work on Mo's hair and the cool clothes Joan picked out for her, there was no mistaking it, even from behind. It was in her walk, the way she held her shoulders, clenched her jaw. Anyone could tell she wasn't right.

Joan said, 'What's in the bag, Harry?'

'Top secret mission kit,' I blurted like a moron.

A motorbike policeman, visor up, glided by.

'Best forget I told you anything, Joan.'

'What, Harry?'

'About the mission kit.'

'What mission kit?'

She glanced at Mo, dead-faced behind her Raybans. She'd need a high power stun gun to get Mo's attention. No-one at home. Nearly walked into that man with a kid on his shoulders, red-haired but the spits of Daniel, waved a flag and laughed and sang, 'I'm two, I'm two!' like two was the best age in your life you could possibly be. I looked again. She wasn't a bit like Dan.

It was easy to get separated in the crush outside Holland Park tube. I nearly managed it, but Joan grabbed my T-shirt and held on while we waited for the green man. That smell I used to like, tar, melting, came up from the road. I could choke on it.

'Hugo!' squeaked an old lady, pushing past us as we did our funeral walk up the little hill to the park.

'Come and jam it with me,' faded off the second we got inside. Seemed like we'd entered another time zone or something. Loads of white people, posh people, foreigners speaking, I don't know, Patagonian, all sorts of crazy languages.

'Hugo, dahling!' squeaked the lady, hobbling up the steep bit like she had one foot in a ditch.

Joan tapped my arm, said quietly, 'Congenital dislocated hip, Harry. CHD for short. Hardly see that now we've got hip replacements.'

She let me in on trade secrets sometimes because if I couldn't be a fireman on account of my trouble with heights I was going to be an orthopaedic surgeon when I grew up.

The lady gripped the fence, bent over to a little dog in a checked jacket that had its nose stuck in some rubbish.

'Hugo! Come away. No winkies for you.'

We crossed the picnic lawn. Women in white karate jim-jams kicked the air. Kids played cricket. We dragged our way through the ornamental gardens. Ranks of flowers stood up and waved like happy soldiers. The fountain giggled water.

We plodded down the steps, around those railings where Daniel got his head stuck seemed like a million years ago. On the café side people laughed, read papers, drank cappuccinos, swatted pigeons away.

'Hello there!' bellowed one of those extra-tall posh men, waving his arms about like he was trying to get a message across a howling storm. His friend – she was only sat behind the railings – stretched her eyes wide, shook her napkin at him, raining crumbs, swept one hand towards the empty chair beside her.

'I wish people would stop it,' Mo said, you wouldn't believe how loud.

'Stop what?' said Joan.

Mo made her mouth into a tight, mean slit, upped the volume.

'Stop flaunting themselves and their happiness and their, their, their bloody premium strollers.'

People stared, looked away. Smack bang in front of us, a woman wrenched her three-wheel buggy round and pushed it back the way she'd come. That showy man pulled a naughty-boy-caught-out face at his friend.

I tried to imagine I was with some other family. The little girl, maybe, in a white dress, ankle socks and shiny red shoes dashing across the path, giggling,

'Daddy, Daddy, I saw a flutterby!'

The trees behind her seemed to whisper glad noises. Happy yellow light bounced off their leaves.

Joan yanked Mo off the path.

'Let's have an ice-cream. Here's a lovely bench.'

It was like all the others, only carved across the top it said, 'Edward and Sarah. Together in life. Together in death.'

I wanted to go with Joan, help her carry, do something, anything, but I had to be a good son, stay, look after Mo.

'So cold,' Mo shivered.

'Freezing,' I said.

It was the hottest Carnival weekend in living memory.

I watched Hugo by the opera steps, a fluffy St Bernard's sniffing his bum. Hugo wagged his tail and laughed like that was the best doggy joke in the world. Mo was right. There was an awful lot of happiness about.

'Vanilla, pistachio, chocolate, take your pick.' Joan held them out.

'Just had breakfast,' Mo lied, not looking up.

I said, 'Chocolate please, mmMMmm, lovely Joan,' to make up for Mo being rude.

Joan forced a gap through Mo's fist, popped the pistachio cornet in.

'Come on, Mo, for me,' I said. 'Just a little lick.'

I caught myself in her Raybans, grinning like a wassock. She took one lick.

'Go on, a bite. For me, Mo. For me.'

It wasn't difficult talking like that once you got the hang of it.

'You eat half, I'll eat the rest for you.'

Pistachio was my second favourite flavour.

The other side of Mo, Joan closed her eyes, took in the sun, head back, her chin pointing at the very spot beyond the tennis courts where Otis once appeared like magic, running to our rescue. I could have told her it wasn't going to be like that this time. Otis wasn't up to it, nor Pa neither.

I took a bite of my ice-cream, it didn't taste nearly as good as it used to.

Putting Mo right – Mo, cramming it in now, not enjoying it, cramming it in, a green drip running down her chin – just putting Mo right was going to take a thousand years at this rate. Something had to be done. Someone had to do it.

Maybe it was a sign or something, that Joan seemed to understand the importance of my mission. Maybe there'd be other signs, I'd best watch out for them. When, felt like hours and hours later, we finally made it to the corner of Terry's street, she touched my shoulder and said,

'You run on up, Harry. We'll see you in from here. Good luck.'

14

'Here's the orders,' Terry said when I got back from the toilet the second time.

We were in the library on huge red leather armchairs, should have been smoking pipes, it was that sort of room, smelled of wax.

Terry leaned right back in his chair, spoke so softly I had to lean in, strain to hear.

'Today's the day. Dennis here. Folks in LA. Consuela in charge. Weather A-I perfect.'

Blood roared in my ears. I don't know if it was Terry in his battle fatigues being so completely fantastic or the Condition Red Alert that did it.

'First, right, you hide in the bushes behind the shed, commando-style, like we practised.'

'Right.'

'Next, I rush over to Dennis, say there's something wrong with Consuela, she's collapsed. Dennis comes back to the house. Right? Then, you search the shed. You're looking nervous, Harry.'

Me, in the shed. All alone.

I tried to rest one elbow on the chair, show how relaxed I felt about it. Missed. Slipped off.

'Brilliant plan, Terry. Just one thing.' My voice came out squeaky. 'What if he comes back?'

Terry was quiet for a bit.

'I thought of that. He'll be tied up here for ages. Everything gets complicated with Consuela. She's from Manila.'

'Right, OK. But . . .'

Terry pushed himself up, walked over to the fireplace, picked up a harmonica from the gigantic white marble mantel piece, blew the first bit of *Here Comes the Bride*.

'You hear this, Dennis is coming. Vamoosh.'

'Va-what?'

'You disappear, Harry.'

'Right. OK. Sure thing.'

'Not straight across the grass, though.'

'No, obviously not, absolutely.'

'Hide in the bushes. Creep back through the cover.'

'Right.' I swallowed hard.

'And, Harry.'

Terry stood, arms folded, legs apart, his back to the fireplace, like he was warming his bum on an invisible fire. Stayed there staring at me so long I nearly asked for the toilet again.

'Harry. Whatever happens, we do not snitch. Got that?'

'What?'

'Snitch. Grass. Fess up. It isn't done. Got it? Not to anyone.'

'No way, no. Absolutely, Terry.'

'This isn't kids' stuff, Harry. You break the code, the SAS are duty-bound to kill you. Not just me. Any member of the battalion has to kill you.'

Oh.

'Stand up.'

I had to steady myself against the chair.

'Comrade's honour,' Terry said.

'Comrade's honour.'

'Pain of death.'

'Absolutely.'

'This is crucial, Harry. Pain of death. You've got to say the words.'

I said them, Pain of Death, while we did this special handshake which involved Terry bending back my pinkie.

'Any questions?'

I gripped my throbbing finger, didn't know if I was supposed to have questions or not.

'What exactly am I looking for?'

He looked at me like I was stupid.

'Anything incriminating.'

'Right, OK. And then what?'

'Whadya mean?'

'What happens next?'

'We watch and wait, Harry. Seize our chance. Lock him in the shed. And do it.'

'Do what, exactly?'

Terry narrowed his eyes. 'You're not turning chicken on me?'

'No, no, course not.'

'Well, Harry, what do you think happens next?'

I cleared my throat. 'Burn it?'

Terry was such a good actor I could believe Consuela had died. He sobbed real tears, trotted ahead of the man, blubbed, 'all red and puffy. Wheezing and everything.'

I watched them disappear into Terry's, whispered, 'Cover me,' made my move.

'I'll cover you,' said Biffo, 'but we shoulda discussed this. Crazy stunt. Crazy. You don't have to go through with it. Believe me, Kid, you're cruisin for a bruisin. Big time.'

Oh, yeah. Like he could tell the future all of a sudden.

The shed door was held shut with one of those wooden pegs you move round. Easy on the dry run. Impossible now it was for real. My hands wobbled, slipped about. Vital seconds ticked away.

I did it and slipped into the dark.

Smelt earth, wood and something chemical.

Walked into something big, warm and heavy like a man. I heard heavy panicked breathing. A hammering heart. I waited for the bad thing to happen.

Nothing happened. It was a bag of earth or something I'd bumped into. I could see that now, my eyes getting used to the dark. A bag of earth. That's all. Must be me, my body, making all that racket.

I could see all sorts now. Rakes, spades, hoes, different shapes and sizes. That bag I'd bumped into, 'Total Lawn Dressing', I counted three more. There was one roll of chicken wire, jaggedy edges. One roll of carpet, a plastic drain pipe, a strip of curtain rail. Everything neat, suspiciously neat. A huge axe head that looked like a propeller.

A harmonica note. Just one.

I stopped breathing, listened for the man, come to get me, axe me over the head and do whatever it was he did to Daniel, if he really was the one who did it.

Nothing. Just the wind.

Remember the basics:

Number one, what was it?

Don't panic, it'll come.

Number two: Permit no distraction.

Number one, oh, yes: Breathe.

uuuuuuuHaaaaaaa.

That's better.

Red Setter twine, a roll too big to lift, a dog on the packet.
A box, 'Galia melons', had something else inside. I couldn't
see what without moving the roll that was too big to lift.
A bundle of sticks, rusty nails in them. A sprayer gun, 'Speed
Weed Spray', one, two, three, four plastic buckets. An awful
lot of gardening gloves. Two glass coffee jars, labels on them,
'dibromide' and 'dichloride'.

Bang! Went the door. *BangBang!* My heart jumped – not
into my mouth like people say, right up my throat.

I grabbed for the door, checked the coast was clear, and
that's when I spotted it.

A chill started at my neck, crept over my head and tugged
my eyebrows up.

On a shelf, behind the door, in a plastic tray, something
that didn't belong.

A pink, fluffy, baby something, hidden away.

Something incriminating.

A child's cardigan, it was, a baby's cardigan, tiny, its buttons delicate and speckled like those little chocolate eggs
Grampy used to send at Easter.

I looked around at ranks of rakes and hoes, the blades
and prickly things, the nasty sprays, the deadly chemicals.
Every single thing in there you could use to hurt a child.

I put the cardigan back. In neat black letters on a label

on the tray I saw the kid's initials I would never forget.

A train rumbled by above Barlby Road. *Yanottinuff*, *Yanottinuff*, *Yanottinuff*, said the train.

I wasn't enough, but I could be.

Fast and full of flat notes, *Here Comes the Bride* flew in on the wind.

I slipped out the door, ran through the bushes, didn't mind my face being scraped. Didn't mind anything.

Killer blades and killer sprays, a baby cardigan in the shed.

Bastard. Dirty bloody bastard.

Had to keep a souvenir.

LP. Poor LP.

Liam Preston?

Luke Potter?

Lucy Peach?

Maybe another kid called Pickles.

Hardly noticed the rain coming down til I was soaked through and shivering.

I looked back to see the gardener walk away from Terry's in a suspicious manner and gather up his tools. The grass smelt sweet. He worked quickly like he knew his time was running out.

15

One thing we tried to do like always that year was drink Grampy's wine. We did it every year, didn't make a fuss or anything, just drank the wine like Grampy had every year since they shot out his eye.

'Will there be a happy birthday cake?' Dan said one time, like an idiot.

'No, love,' said Mo.

'It's more a way of remembering,' said Pa, 'remembering Grampy's –'

'Eye?'

Mo said, 'Not exactly, Dan Dan.'

'Remembering the courage of the Catalans?'

'Exactly, yes, well said, Harry,' said Pa. I smiled at Daniel.

'You see, Dan, it takes courage to fight,' said Pa. 'And Grampy was just a boy. And he was miles and miles from home. And no-one made him go. He did it because he thought it was right. He'd never been abroad. And, losing an eye, darling, that's a dreadful thing. And still he stayed and he fought, like –'

'Like a war hero?' I said.

Pa said, 'Yes, Harry, that's right. Exactly like a war hero.'

I smiled at Daniel. He smiled back, like an idiot.

This time, Pa rummaged upstairs for the wine. It was special red stuff, dusty and old. Grampy had had it forever. Pa always said if it was in the shops, which it wouldn't be, there's no way you could afford it, not even a glass.

Joan stood at the window trying to shut out the *boom judda judda* from the sound systems.

'You shouldn't be doing that, babe,' said Otis, hands on her hips so firm her dress moved up a bit. 'Let me.'

Pa came in holding the bottle. He looked sadder than usual.

'It's the very last one.'

Joan took her place at the window end of the table, buttered her bread, knocked her water back, poured herself another from the jug.

'Mission accomplished, Harry?'

My ears went hot. I grunted something that gave nothing away and passed her the Brie. I budged up for Otis, on my side. He squeezed in beside Pa, on the other.

Joan said, 'Just a drop for me thanks, Dom,' which wasn't like her. Pa splashed some in my water.

I said, 'Thanks, Pa,' which was nice of me because I knew from last time it was pukey. I tucked into my bread and my favourite hummus Joan had brought. It was good eating food that was new.

Mo, at the dark end of the table under the scary Picasso, rolled a baby tomato about on her plate. Joan must have helped her dress. She had on proper clothes, not like a person, though. More like a shop window dummy, or a doll.

'Feelin better today, babe?' Otis said, like Joan had been poorly.

'Grand, thanks, babe.' She cut herself a huge chunk of Brie, squashed the whole of it onto her bread. Otis bounced a warning look off her.

'Oh,' Joan whispered. 'A little bit won't matter.'

A little bit!

I said, 'Pa, is it true about Grampy?'

'What about Grampy, honey?' He leaned towards Mo with the bottle. She put her hand over her glass.

'About Grampy killing people.'

'Harry, please. Not that. You know, Otis, I can't seem to get that punching right.'

'But, did he, really, Pa?'

'Not *at* the bag, *through* the bag,' Otis said. 'Technique, Dom. Work and practice.'

Pa took a whole smoked mackerel and made a doorstep sandwich. He wasn't being greedy. He was eating for the tapeworm, too.

'Pa, did he?'

'Did who do what, Harry?' Talking with his mouth full.

'Did Grampy kill people?'

'Harry, please.'

Otis gave Joan that look again. A whole secret conversation going on in front of us. Mo picked up on it, glared at her plate like she'd burn holes right through it and the table.

'But, Pa, I need to know.' I really did. There might be a sign in it.

'Harry, I never asked him. He fought in a war. It was a just war.'

Joan gave Otis her bread and Brie and a smile.

'It's not always wrong to kill people, is it Pa?'

'Harry! Please! Some other time.'

Joan gulped back gallons of water.

'But, Pa, if Grampy killed the bad guys, and he was fighting for the good guys, then that was all right, wasn't it?'

Pa dragged a hand across his face.

'Sometimes it's the least bad thing to do. Grampy was a brave man. A very good man. I never knew him do or say a cruel or nasty thing.'

I looked at the Picasso, the dead man at the front, his eyes all over, his arms flung wide, his sword completely shattered.

Joan let out a belch, and giggled, covered her mouth.

'Oops! Sorry, folks.'

Mo crashed her fork down on her plate.

'Why don't you just put out a press release?'

'What?' said Joan. 'What do you mean?'

'You might as well announce it, you've made it so bloody obvious.'

It wasn't obvious to me.

Joan said, 'It's too soon for that, Mo. It's very early.'

Pa glanced from Joan to Otis to the Brie, back to Joan again. You could almost hear a clunky penny drop.

'Otis, Joan, this is the best news!'

I said, 'What news?'

Crash went the butter dish we bought in St Ives.

Mo stood up, shrieked, 'Piling into the Brie as if you didn't know.'

140

Otis breathed out hard through his nose, said, 'There's no cause for this, Mo, no cause at all.'

Joan stopped him with a stare.

Mo banged on, 'And you a nurse, for God's sake!'

'Mo, stop it!' Pa's voice cracked.

Otis pushed up. Joan touched his hand. Otis sat down again.

'Flaunting it, flaunting it,' Mo sobbed. 'I suppose *you* knew about this.'

She picked up Grampy's wine, gripped it round the neck.

'I only guessed,' Pa said, 'when you did.'

He moved to take the bottle. She swept it back. Red splashed that scary picture with the woman screeching just like Mo.

'You knew!'

'I didn't know.'

'There's more to it, isn't there?'

'What?'

Mo hurled Grampy's bottle at the dishwasher. Glass skittered about. Wine splashed like blood across the floor and up the yellow wall.

I said, 'What's going on, please?'

Seemed no-one heard me, then Otis murmured, 'Joanie's expecting, Harry.'

'Expecting what?'

He closed his eyes. 'A baby, mate.'

'But, that's a good thing, isn't it?'

Joan ruffled my hair. 'It's a very good thing, thank you, H.'

Any minute she was going to cry.

Mo snarled, 'Don't touch him!'

Joan snatched her hand away. Tears spilled out of her.

Pa reached out to Mo. From the back of his throat he groaned, 'Mo! Please, Mo!'

Mo pushed him away, dashed through the door, slammed it and thundered up the stairs.

You could have counted to twenty in the silence after that. Otis sat, eyes closed, did his special breathing trick to make himself calm. Joan paced and blew her nose. Pa stood in a bloody puddle, stone still and grey, a dead man with the stiffness setting in.

Joan said, 'It's all right. It's all right.'

But it wasn't all right and it wouldn't be all right until someone did something to sort it.

I called Terry like he'd told me to.

Brrring brrring.

'Hello?'

'Is Terry there?'

'Terry who? I think you've got the wrong number, Miss.'

Miss?

I punched the number, carefully this time.

Brrring brrring. I realised I was actually holding my breath.

'Hola?' He said Consuela always got stuff wrong.

'Is Terry there?'

'One moment.'

I heard her shoes clack clack clack. I closed my eyes and saw Consuela in her crisp blue uniform walk down the white marble hallway. She held a giant silver tray. In the middle, a special creamy coloured card, 'Harry Pickles, calling', written on with one of those old fashioned pens. I watched her tiptoe up the stairs so as not to disturb him, knock softly on his door, straighten her white apron, smooth her hair and wait.

In real life she stayed right by the phone and screeched, 'Terry! Phone for you!'

He yelled something back at her, I couldn't hear what.

'Why should I have a damn!' Consuela shouted. 'Iss your fren. Come now, Terry! Vamos! You wan I hang up? Or what?'

I heard him running down the stairs.

'You forgetta something?'

I heard a voice like Terry's, but not his real one, 'Er, no, I don't think . . .'

'Boy, I tellin you, you forgetta something.'

'Oh,' he said, 'oh, thank you, Consuela.'

'Thank you my ass,' she said. Her footsteps clacked away.

Down the phone came Terry's real voice, but quietly: 'Yeah, right, Harry. Don't know what's got into her. Must be her time of the month. Now, listen carefully, Pickles. Plan B. I've got the new orders here.'

16

Whistles split the air. I saw a great fat tongue push into a neat little mouth, right in front of me. Fat and pink and downright rude. She didn't mind, that white woman, bleached mop of hair, funny cigarette behind one ear, everything pierced. She didn't mind, no, she was eating his face. Barbecue smoke itched my eyes. Heavy-beated music boom-boomed against my chest, filled my head.

FEELIN SEX SEX-EE.

Terry tugged my sleeve. I shook him off.

'See? There!' Terry yelled. 'It's him! It's him!'

That woman gripped the black man by his hair, shoved more of his face into her mouth. Her other hand dropped, grabbed him hard. Down there. Must've hurt. The man pushed his thigh between her legs, slid a hand down, pushed one finger hard against her bum hole. Right there in the street!

'Harry, are you paying attention! I'm telling you, it's him!'

Mo and Pa would murder me if they knew. It isn't safe at the Carnival Monday night. Sound systems wreck your hearing. People get stabbed. Serve them right if I got deafed or killed. Should've thought of that before Pa stole Otis, before Mo smashed Grampy's wine and wrecked Joan's surprise.

'I say we do him here!' yelled Terry.

Up ahead, another sound system pumped,

JUMP AND WAVE, JUMP UP AND WAVE.

People did what the song told them to.

SEX, SEX-EE, crashed into JUMP AND WAVE.

'Harry!' Terry shouting into my eardrum now. 'Harry! I said, have you got the weapon?'

Beats and words and people bashed together. People slipped on lumps of burgers, chicken wings, corncobs, people slipped and slid about. Forgot about their feet, stretched their hands high. Didn't care about their armpits or anything. Jumped. Jumped and waved.

'Harry! Listen to me!'

Sod Mo. Sod Pa. Sod them. I wasn't their boy. Jerk chicken juices sticky on my face, gravelly burnt bits smeared across my Wild Boy T-shirt, Mr Fantastic, that's me, down the Carnival with my mate.

Just off Portobello, Terry was pointing. Outside the Warwick Castle, in front of a police barrier, a white man leaned into a dustbin. A cardboard sign next to him, soggy and torn, said, 'Cold bear £1.50'. He looked like a bear, actually.

'Harry. You stupid or what?'

JUMP AND WAVE, JUMP UP AND WAVE.

You've maybe never been to the Carnival. Imagine you're in a boxing ring. A hundred sweaty people packed in with you. The music feels like boxers in front of you, boxers behind you, boxers all round you, hammering at your head. Imagine it. Absolutely bloody brilliant!

The crowd swept us on.

Terry yelled, 'Pickles! That's your target! You know the orders. Do him.'

The man looked a lot like the bus driver. Not so much like the gardener, though.

'Makes you think, don't it, Kid?' Bloody Biffo. Who invited him along?

'But, Terry –'

'You're not turning chicken –'

'No, no, it's just, maybe –'

You had to cut everything down at the Carnival, scream it out, else you'd never get heard above the noise. 'It's just, you know, plan our strategic approach.' I'm not sure he heard any of that. 'Round the block!'

Maybe if I could get Terry away for a bit that man might move on and that would be a sign, wouldn't it, that maybe we should wait. It's kind of final, isn't it, killing a person?

Seemed like Terry was thinking about my round the block strategy when a train of boy-men chanting, chugged towards us, baggy trousers loose round their hips, Calvin Klein boxer tops peeking over. The toughest boys had their flies slung open. They were lords of the Carnival, special and scary. You had to give way to them, bend your body, let them by.

'Terry! Look out!'

Terry, log-like.

'Terry! Move!'

Shocked, frightened or something.

Terry disappeared.

The boy-men train chugged on.

I had to heave him to his feet.

'I can handle it,' he said.

Obviously he couldn't. He was shaking. I tugged him out of the crowd and into Woolies' doorway.

'Take a breather. Hands on your knees. Get your head down or you'll faint. That's it, Terry. Well done.'

Seemed Terry had vanished with his colour. Pale, smaller looking, kind of pathetic. I was thinking we might call it a night, go home, forget the man til some other day. I patted him on his shoulder.

'Feeling a bit better now?'

Big mistake.

Terry stood up straight, spat, shook himself. His colour came back and so did his self.

'Stop fussing. Nothing wrong with me. Just lost my footing.'

Brushed muck off his battle fatigues.

'Right. Orders. Let's do him here. Yeah, yeah, let's get the dirty bastard.'

'Yeah. Right. Let's nip round the block, first. You know, plan our –'

'Seize the moment,' he said, then he grabbed me and tugged me back along the shop fronts til we got a good view of the man.

Mister Boombastic came over from the sound system.

Biffo said, 'Now, hold on here, I –'

I said, 'But, Terry. The police!'

Two coppers leaned against the barrier, trying to blend in in their luminous green vests. They joshed their mate – he was dancing with an old black lady, you know, like they do to make up for the rest of the year.

'You're not backing out on me now, Harry?'

'Course not.'

'We're in this together. Comrade's honour.'

He held my arm so tight his nails dug in. He gripped

me in his cold blue eyes like he was trying to scare me from the inside out.

'Comrade's honour, Harry.'

Freeze my blood.

'Comrade's honour, Terry.'

'Pain of death.'

'Pain of death, Terry.'

'Dirty bloody bastard. You mustn't let him get away with it.'

'No, right, sure thing.'

That man, something in the curve of his back. Imagine what Terry'd think if I didn't even try. Cluck cluck, that's what.

'You can't let Daniel down again,' he said. 'Open the knife and do it, Harry.'

Biffo said, 'Now, listen up, Kid —'

Those drum men drowned him out.

BADA-BADA-BOOM-BOOM! BADA-BADA-BOOM! Raw. Fresh. Angry.

Let Daniel down again.

'Think what he did, Harry.'

I tried to think of something, anything else. I thought of Grampy, marching into battle with the drums, of Mo and Pa, the never-ending row, Joan's angry tears, the bottle smashed, the something that had to be done. It was late. I felt wrecked. It was hard to keep your thoughts all in a line.

'Think what he did.'

Bright clear pictures hit my brain, blasted every thought away.

'Think, Harry.'

A train rumbled over Portobello Road.

Yanottinuff, Yanottinuff, Yanottinuff, said the train.

I clicked open the dagger. I wasn't enough, but I was going to be.

'Go for it, Pickles,' Terry said as he legged it. 'Meet you by the bogs.'

I moved into the crowd, right arm pinned to my side, blade pointing down. Marched, marched, through the crowds, could hardly see for tears, marched, marched like Grampy marching into battle with the drums.

Mister Boombastic started doing his thing. My song, that was. Had to be a sign.

The dancing policeman sang along, ground his hips. His mates had a great laugh. Mister Boombastic getting all romantic now. That lady did a super-quick smile, backed off and made her getaway.

I passed the man, turned hard and moved in on him, my back to the policemen.

Terry, by the toilets, went jab jab jab with his arm.

Light bounced off a white roll of flesh just above the man's bum.

For Daniel. For Daniel.

Something had to be done.

I turned my face away, closed my eyes and pulled my arm back. Is this how you do it? Punch, punch, punch the blade in?

Something held me back.

'What you doing, son? You'll cut yourself. Put that away.'

An old black guy, shirt open to his trousers, beer and smoke on his breath, had hold of my arm.

'You shouldn't be out nights, boy like you. Where's your

mother? Where's your mother, son? Stop shaking, boy. I'm not gonna hurt you.'

I opened my mouth. A small whine came out.

'Give me that there here.'

He took the weapon, clicked the dagger back, folded it, dropped it in my pocket.

'Keep that in there before you get yourself arrested. Go home, boy. Home, before I turn you in myself.'

People crowded in on me, sucked my energy out.

I stumbled towards the bogs, searched for Terry in the dark. My face filled up with snot and tears.

'Pickles! Holy shit! You had me going, you really had me going!'

'What?'

My legs went.

'Hell's teeth! Shit!'

He was looking kind of scared and angry and excited all at once. I didn't get it, couldn't put the pieces all together.

'You would've done, wouldn't you? You really would've done it!'

'But I didn't, Terry.'

'What? You kill me, Pickles! You really kill me! You've passed the test. You've won the forfeit. The weapon's yours for life.'

'But, what what what about the man? What what about LP?'

'LP?'

'The kid.'

'The kid?' He looked at me like I was stupid, then got his face real close and shouted into mine, 'LP, Harry. Sound familiar? LP, think about it. Lost Property, Pickles, I should say. Lost Property. Don't you think?'

I couldn't think. I didn't want to think, not now, not ever, never again. My heart seemed to twist. Never had Chinese burns inside before.

Back to school

17

I nipped in to fill my lunch box. Mo flicked through that catalogue so fast she nearly dropped it.

'Sorry, Mo. Didn't mean to make you jump.'

'Jump? Me. No. Just looking. Something for Joan.'

She'd been looking at the baby pages. I seen her.

'Joan wouldn't be seen dead in that.'

'Ah, now, pinafores aren't really her, are they? Yes. Yes. You're right there, Harry. Perhaps I'll send her . . .'

Mo shut the catalogue, put her hands on top of it, sat statue-still, eyes closed. These days she did a lot of that.

I thought of the time Dan saw a baby catalogue, asked could you really get one through the post like that.

'Oh, yes, Dan,' said Mo, with a big boy's wink for me. 'Can you imagine, Dan Dan, the trouble Mr Posty had getting you two through the letter box?'

In the fridge I found an exploded yoghurt. No juice.

'Why send her anything?'

'What? Oh, that. It'd be nice, Harry.'

'I mean, why *send* it. Why not give it her yourself?'

'Ah, well, now.' She picked at her nails.

On my treats and biscuits shelf I caught my finger on

the sharp corner of a box. Long and slim. Across the top it said, 'Clear Plan Home Ovulation Test.' Two silver envelopes inside. I closed my eyes, said – ov-you-lay-shun – stamped the shape of it on my tongue, and moved to Daniel's shelf. Dust and sardines.

I don't know how long since Mo had scared Joan and Otis off. Weeks and weeks I hadn't seen them. Not since the Carnival and here we were at school already. Brilliant work, Mo. Top marks.

Hey! Blueberry jam! Jam sandwiches, that'd be nice!

Mo barked, 'Football!'

I banged my funny bone on the bread bin.

No bread in it, just half a cream cracker that was bendy.

'What about it, Mo?'

'Today, last lesson, isn't it? Football in the park?'

'Well, yes.'

'I'll be there.'

'Pa too?' Stupid question. You know those men – quiet lodger types that keep to their selves and don't speak to you or look you in the eye or say Honey or Sweet Boy or even Harry any more, and turn out to be serial killers or enemy spies? Well, Pa was like that.

'Just me.'

'You'll freeze in the park.'

'Looks like a lovely warm day, Harry.'

'It'll be dark.'

'It'll be grand.'

Seemed skipping and boxing was all Pa did at home. And the row. I could do it for them – I'm thirty-nine. But it's grotesque, Mo – save them the trouble. What was it Pa said last time? Reaching out over the mess,

'Mo, Mo,' or 'No, No,' or 'No, Mo.'

Then, hard and clear, like the voice on the underground that tells you to:

Mind. The. Gap.

What was it he said exactly?

'Mo. Please. Don't. Drive. Me. Away.'

I said, 'But you're not used to going out, Mo.'

'Well it's time I got used to it. Life goes on, Harry.'

Then she did that eyes closed sitting still thing again. I took a banana. It was mushy and black, but it was either that or the satsuma in the green furry coat.

My advice to you is, right, if something ever happens to you or your brother, say, that's so big that everyone at school is talking about you, the thing to do is, right, stay out of the bogs.

'Give him space,' said Terry, banging the door open so it bashed against the wall. No way could I get my poo done now. I stuck the comic under my arm and pulled up my feet so you couldn't see them under the cubicle door.

'You what?' said Piggy. Lots of unzipping.

'Space,' said Terry. 'Time to work through his ishoos.'

Sounded like they were both peeing now.

'What kind of talk is that?' said Piggy.

Pete – so he was there – said, 'I think what Terry's saying is treat him carefully. You know, he's in shock and –'

'Invite him round and stuff,' said Piggy.

'Yeah,' said Pete. 'Get your mum to put on one of her nice teas and –'

'I don't think you're hearing me,' said Terry.

'Bad luck,' said Piggy.

'Too right,' said Pete.

'No, I mean, bad luck you guys. Mine's the highest. Then you, Pete. And Terry, well –'

'We weren't competing, then,' said Terry, zipping up. 'Permit no distraction. Remember? We were talking about –'

'It's agreed. We ask him round and give him cake and stuff,' said Piggy. 'I'm still the winner.'

'You're not hearing me,' said Terry. 'We need to give him space. Give him time to work through all his ishoos.'

'What kind of hippie talk is that?' said Piggy.

'You watch your mouth, Piggy. What I'm saying is until further notification you know who is out of the gang.'

'But –'

'No buts, Piggy. No buts in soldiering.'

I heard running water and a lot of splashing. Piggy, I bet, washing his hands really rough to show his anger, his pouty face all wobbly. But what did Pete have to say about it? I mean, he was my best mate and everything and you don't dump your best mate just because he's got ishoos.

'It's time for geography.' That's what Pete said and that's all he said and they scarpered.

I ought to try to have my poo, then pull myself together. A little bit of time, that's what I needed.

More guys came in, two of them, big guys from top class, I don't know their names.

'They never iz found my mum says.'

'Yeah.'

You could hear them unzipping. I put my feet down,

opened my comic, made what could turn out to be an important discovery for medical science.

'Or they iz found dead.'

The sound of pee, one first, then the other joining in.

What happened was, the Bash Street Kids' teacher decided to ignore them, no matter how bad they were.

'Yeah. Dead more like it.'

The Kids did their usual stuff, you know, throwing fruit at the blackboard, playing music loud, eating buns and all that.

'Raked.'

'Yeah . . . Wossat?'

What happened next was, the teacher, well . . .

'You know, raked. They iz always raked.'

'Yeah. Raked . . . Nasty.'

I heard those big boys zip up.

'Very nasty.'

Stupid comic. My important discovery, which might help you if you're a medical scientist or something, is, you can't cry and poo at the same time.

One arm, dark and hairy, touched my shoulder, her hand resting on my desk. I smelt her warmth.

'I'm proud of you, Harry Pickles.'

'It means wailing or howling, Miss.'

'I beg your pardon?'

'Ululations, Miss.'

I thought she was proud of me on account of I was using the big dictionary. We got pizza points for expanding our vocabulary at break time and when we'd saved up enough we could have pizza and juice in the gym. Hooray! With Mr Donald. Boo!

'Look, Miss. It says widows do it.'

She put her glasses on and read where I was pointing.

'Mmmm. So it does.'

I said, 'Mo does a lot of ululating.'

'I should expect so.'

'Not Pa, though.'

'And what about you, Harry?'

'Me? No, Miss. Boys don't.'

'Oh, I know boys who cry, Harry. Men too.'

I turned around to see if she was for real. I had imagined Miss Bliss spent her free time marking homework and traipsing round museums. Miss Bliss knew men. Who cried.

'It's brave to cry sometimes.'

'Yeah, but I just don't, Miss.'

I turned back to the dictionary.

She said, 'I should consider it a brave thing to do.'

I thought of Otis gulping back To Have And To Hold.

'Sometimes I do.'

'Good for you.'

'In my sleep, Miss.'

Her knees creaked like she was getting up to go.

I wanted to keep her.

It was nice being alone with Miss Bliss. There were all sorts of things I could ask her. Like, was it Daniel missing that was putting my mates off me? Or was it me who had changed? Could I change myself back? Would I be able to walk round school again one day thinking, I don't know, normal things? About My Sissay's soft black curls. Or what's for lunch. Or isn't Kylie a moron. Or would it always be this way? In the toilets, at the water fountain, round the merit board, everywhere I went, jamming my thoughts like enemy radar: Daniel Isn't Here.

No way would I ask her those things, obviously not, but I could do if I had to and there was something nice about that.

She moved away.

'About ululations, Miss. I mean, you're either ululating or you're not. What would a person be wanting with a test kit?'

'An ul-ul-a-tion test kit?'

'Yes.'

'Oh.'

She was quiet for a bit. My tummy rumbled.

'You may find you're mistaken, Harry. There is such a thing as an ov-you-lay-shun test. That's something quite different.'

'Can I look it up, Miss?'

'You may.'

She walked over to her desk. I raced her, found it, ovulation, just as she sat down.

'Formation of ova or ovules,' I told her.

'Cast your mind back to last term's science topic.'

It didn't help.

'Do you recall ovulation in female mammals?'

Blood rushed to my face.

'Oh, that.'

'Yes, that,' she said.

I felt a total wassock.

'TWENTY BURPEES!' We all groaned and got down on the wet grass. Mr Donald marched like a drill sergeant along the front row.

Piggy, at the back with me, whispered, 'Call that a PRESS-up?'

Mr Donald shouted, 'Call that a PRESS-up, Kahn? Start at NUMber ONE!'

Piggy panted, 'You should COUNT your LUCKY STARS, boys.'

Mr Donald yelled, 'You should COUNT your LUCKY STARS, boys.'

He always said that because if it hadn't been for the knee-shattering tackle that ended his career he'd be a retired international by now and we'd be messing around like a bunch of disorganised boys instead of doing running pairs and circuits and burpees and all the stuff he made us do before we ever got to play footie.

Piggy whispered, 'That's a BUNNY hop, not a SQUAT thrust. SHAPE up, HUP Hup.'

Mr Donald yelled, 'WAKE UP, EVANS!'

'Two out of three, eh, Picks.'

'Fifty percent,' I said.

Piggy was on great form until we got to running pairs and he started up that song that goes,

'You're not singing. You're not singing. You're not singing any more.'

Only what he sang was,

'Whiffy Harry and his shirt.'

Biffo warned me about my shirt. I was fed up with him nagging me.

We pulled up, wheezing and coughing. Mr Donald made Terry and Peter captains on account of their Excellent Rapport in one-twos. Piggy started up his Whiffy Shirt song under his breath so I kicked him.

Piggy snapped, 'Fuck it, Picks! Where's your sense of humour?'

He must have answered himself because he muttered, 'Sorry, Picks,' and waddled off, leaving me all on my own which was almost worse than having Piggy next to me singing about my stupid smelly shirt.

Peter and Terry pulled on their black armbands.

I wasn't expecting Terry to pick me. Peter, though. I had hopes of Peter.

He picked Jason Smith, then Adrian Mahoney – Pete high-fived him. Terry got the McNally twins. You can't be hanging around long after those guys, not if you're premier league. I hacked a hole in the mud with my heel. Kicked my shin by mistake. It really hurt.

Peter picked Brian Smith, his leg still strapped over the popped patella he got off Piggy on Sports Day. Still, he'd do in goal. Scurfy Murphy. Totally useless. Then – can you believe it? – Joshua Bernstein. I mean, like, really. Speccy Bernstein.

Terry looked at me.

I tapped my chest and nodded at him.

Who? Me?

He wagged his finger, pointed behind me.

No, him.

Piggy? No way.

Piggy.

Terry picked Piggy when he could have had me.

What was it about Daniel gone made them think I couldn't kick straight?

'Are you deaf, Harry Pickles?'

'Yes, Mr Donald. I mean No, Sir.'

Lads laughed but tried to stop themselves.

What's that? Fantastic! Peter picked me!

I pelted over.

'Thanks, Pete.'

He looked at me, like, social death or what?

I said, 'Any chance of striker?'

Pete said, 'I thought I'd give that a go,' his eyebrows saying how he really felt about it. 'We could do with some speed in midfield, though.'

Kind of him to say it that way.

'PaCHEko, are you PICKing your team or conDUCTing a roMANCE?' yelled Mr Donald.

Peter blushed so hard his legs went darker. I'd make it up to him. I'd been practising in my head. I'd swing in soaring crosses to Peter's running feet. I'd be David Beckham to Peter's Michael Owen. We'd be bloody brilliant.

We're keeping possession. Peter gets a shot on goal. *Bang*. Off the cross bar. Adrian heads it back – straight into Sunny's arms. We're doing all right. We need one lucky break.

Sunny does a stonking goal kick deep into our half. I scoop it up, dribble it round both McNallys, push to the halfway line.

Peter's running into space ahead of me,

'My ball! My ball!'

I spot Sunny off his line.

Peter's shouting, 'My ball!'

Sunny's way off his line.

I'm thinking David Beckham. That high, looping ball of his from exactly this position. Remember how it soared and dipped behind the keeper? *Smack!* Into the net.

'Harry! My Ball!'

Beckham did it. Why not me?

'Harry, you twat-head!'

I find out why not.

This time there's a high ball, I'm in space, underneath it, last man before the keeper.

I could play safe. Chest it, trap it, clear it.

'Harry! Time, time,' shouts Peter.

Or I can make up for that other business, do something cool. Yeah. I can head this. I'm brilliant in the air.

Jesus, that hurts.

Ball bounces off the back of my head.

I spin round. Terry's got the ball. He's running at the goal. Brian spreads himself wide. Terry takes a shot.

Bam!

Brian saves it — *Crunch!*

With his dodgy leg.

Terry takes up the rebound.

Bam!

Brian saves it — *Smack!*

With his face.

'Nice one, Bri!'

Brian looks my way. Dizzied.

Terry gathers up the rebound, puts the ball away, punches the air, pulls his shirt over his head, does the crazy chicken.

'Steady ON!' bawls Mr Donald. 'This isn't MATCH of the DAY.'

I don't like to tell you what Brian says to me.

'Sorry, Pete,' I said, when it was over. 'Don't know what's wrong with me.'

Three nil down, it was. You could say I played a part in all their goals.

'S'all right,' Peter said.

The muscle in his jaw that twitched when he was angry, that muscle said it wasn't all right.

'Word of advice, Pickles. Never apologise. Never explain,' Terry, running by. 'Tomorrow, my place?'

Me? Fantastic!

'Yeah, yeah, I'll be there, Tel,' Pete called after him.

Not me.

Piggy waddled past. 'Hey, Tel! Gonna be a bit late.' I didn't catch the rest of it.

'Harry!' Terry shouted back at me.

'Yeah!'

'Isn't that your mum over there?'

He was pointing at the bag lady behind the café railings. Mo, all right. She opened up her newspaper and disappeared behind it.

'Nah. Mo's in Ireland at the moment.'

'Oh,' said Terry. 'See ya, then.'

Peter gave me a look, but I don't think he'd have grassed me up.

'You take care,' he said and then he ran to join the guys.

So, come Saturday and how many other Saturdays already,

Terry, Pete and Piggy too would be climbing our hollow tree and shouting Yabba-Dabba-Doo! Who had I been kidding? I was not premier league. I was not even in the relegation zone. I had slipped down, down, down into the land of muddy pitches and fat-bellied forwards. I was Chester City. I was Rochdale. I was Shrewsbury Town.

I watched them rush away. Terry found a pebble, did an action replay of his goal, crazy chicken and everything. The whole gang, Terry, Pete and Piggy too, shot through the arch into the ornamental gardens and I counted to a hundred in case one of them came back.

Mr Donald touched my shoulder.

'Take heart, Pickles. The best of us lose form sometimes.'

I could have told him that we knew. The knee-shattering tackle that ended his career? Adrian's dad told Adrian who told the rest of us. It didn't happen in England youth squad like Mr Donald said. Oh, no. It didn't happen at all. What happened was he slipped on ice on Hackney Marshes when he was all washed up already.

'Harry, your shirt's a bit whiffy,' Mo said, louder than she meant to, probably. 'Come on, sit down. I've got your favourite.'

Hot chocolate, no froth. Plum tart, Dan's favourite.

'Triffic. Thank you, Mo.'

'Things are going to change round here,' she said.

She'd painted her nails, her lovely nails, bitten down and torn and purple now. She'd washed her hair. You could see all the frizzy ends. She'd put some clothes on that she used to wear, nice clothes I liked. She couldn't fill them any more.

Like in the old days, meeting me, she'd gone to a bit of trouble. But the trouble she'd gone to only made my throat ache.

'How was the game?'

I chewed Dan's tart.

'Three nil.'

'Good man.'

Behind her two men played chess with hardly any pieces on the board. They both had baldy heads and long grey ponytails, faded hippie denims. Brothers, I bet. The younger one moved his castle, sat back and smiled like he'd done something really clever.

The older one said, 'Sssweeet,' like he didn't mind one bit, reached out a hand and touched his brother's cheek.

I swigged my chocolate. It was cold.

'Things are going to change,' Mo said.

The winner rolled a cigarette, passed it to his brother, made another for himself. They leaned together. The happy loser struck a match. They cupped all their hands together, shielded the flame. They drew back, sucked on their cigarettes, closed their eyes and held their breath and then, in perfect time, they breathed out long and happily.

A woman with a baby in one of those big old-fashioned prams rushed at us and yammered something.

'Grand. Yes. Sure,' said Mo. 'My pleasure. On the contrary. Delighted.'

That woman legged it up the café steps. Must have been a foreigner, or bonkers, leaving her baby with a mad lady and a smelly boy.

I said, 'We actually lost the football, Mo.'

'Well done. Good man.' Her eyes stuck to the baby.

'Two goals definitely down to me.'

'At this rate you'll win the cup.'

The baby scrunched its face up, squeaked then cried.

'I think I've lost my touch, Mo.'

She stood up, unzipped something on the pram – don't they have locks? – and took the baby out.

I said, 'Mo, I don't think . . .' but I didn't know how to finish it.

She wasn't listening, anyway. She was doing the hip-swaying thing women do with babies.

'Look at you,' she murmured. 'Look at yooooo.'

She held it close, cooed into its howling face. Her whole body seemed to melt back into Mo again, the happy Mo. It hurt my eyes.

Behind that bit of railing, still not quite straight, where Otis's heavy boot had once touched Daniel's baby hair, a posh lady with a bike was telling a policeman,

'Sweetie, have a heart. I was only pushing it along.'

'I saw you in the saddle, Madam. This is not a laughing matter.'

I said, 'Oh, look, Mo, a policeman.'

'Goorgeous, goorgeous.' She had the baby cooing with her.

My head throbbed with lack of air.

Those brothers cleared away their pieces, blew tobacco off their board.

The mother came back. Mo handed her the baby. They said the gushy stuff that women say. I slumped into my seat and breathed.

The policeman took the lady's name. That stopped her laughing.

Mo sat, eyes closed, very still.

I watched the chess-players breeze round the tables. The happy loser held the gate open, touched his little brother on the hand as he went through, said something and they laughed. I wondered if he'd ever banged his brother's head against the bathroom wall when they were boys.

18

I opened the door. It was Daniel!

'Twick or tweet!'

Daniel, in his Spiderman mask, bouncing out of the night!

I tried to speak. My thumping heart in the way.

He backed off. Nervous.

'Twick or tweet?'

Not Daniel. Not a bit like him.

I slammed the door.

Stupid. Stupid of me. Like he's the only kid with a Spiderman mask.

Out of me tore a howl. An animal's that got its leg snapped in a trap.

Fists pounded the door.

That buzzing felt good in my head so I banged it some more. Harder, harder til the other pain faded, the pain that stopped me breathing, pooing, thinking straight, the empty, empty place that Daniel could fill in one second if he wanted, if he would only come back.

We didn't do Halloween that year. Bonfire Night came and went without us.

'Things are going to change,' Mo kept saying.

But they didn't. We stayed sad, sad, sad.

I grew old, like it was years and not months that were passing.

That time things didn't feel nearly as bad as they should? They felt bad enough now.

That kid who played killing games all summer long? Stupid idiot. Lucky idiot.

Now I knew. Truth was, I could do nothing. There was nothing I could do.

December came and took Pa's mother away. Then, things changed.

Last time I seen her was that hot sticky summer when Dan was a baby and Grampy a skeleton. We took a whole entire day to get there on the world's longest motorway, me and Dan pulling faces at grumpy drivers stood by their cars on the hard shoulder with their bonnets up, sizzling.

'Ah Ssssidney, pet,' she said, showering me with spit soon as I'd got in the door. 'You always wass the most hand-ssome of lads.'

She gripped my face in cold bony fingers. I pulled away from her kisses.

'It's Harry.'

Sidney was Grampy's real name.

She pulled me back.

'You too, Harry, pet.'

And she kissed me again. I couldn't tell if those brown marks on her skin were dirt or the lurgy.

First chance I got I was off up her stairs to wash my face clean. She'd put six dead daisies in a jar by the sink.

The bathroom smelt of Dettol. It was filthy, though. I dried my face with loo paper on account of the stink from her towels.

Back in the dining room it felt hot as Morocco. Daniel wriggled and wheezed at the table, a pile of cushions squashed behind his back. Mo pulled at his sweatshirt, blew down his chest.

'We need to cool him.'

Granma shoved in one more cushion. Dan coughed.

Granma said, 'Now, Deirdre, isn't that better?'

'Mo,' said Mo.

'No? Well, young lady, you are welcome to try and do better.'

'It's a grand job, really. I was only saying, Gran, my name is Mo.'

'I'm not losing track, Deirdre, whatever you may think. Observe.'

Granma stepped back, stretched her arms high, swept them down and got her hands flat on the floor. Her upside-down face turning purple, she said,

'I've got all my own teeth.'

'Help!' Mo's eyes screamed across the room to where Pa stood looking useless and sad.

He wiped his sweaty face. 'Mam, you wouldn't let me turn the fire down, would you?'

The gas fire roared. Out in the street boys in swimming trunks raced around, hurling buckets of water.

Granma got right way up, straightened her shell suit.

'I've been called a few things in my time Dominic, but really!'

'The fire, Mam! The fire!' he shouted.

'Oh, the fire! Why didn't you say so, pet? No, no. I'll not have you econo-mono-mising on my account. What would Deirdre say about that?'

'Mo!' Pa shouted.

'No, what, sweetheart?' Granma shouted back at him.

'Mo, Mam. Mo's not the fussy one. You're thinking of Deirdre, Kevin's wife.'

'Kevin who, pet?'

'Cousin Kevin.'

'Well, I don't know what Cousin Kevin's missis is doing calling me a liar.'

'No, Mother. Nobody's calling you a liar.'

'I should think not. Kevin should have chosen better.'

'Oh, Mam!' Pa said. 'What a lovely spread!'

Granma brightened. She smiled down on her cracked, dirty plates piled with funny-looking lettuce and something pink like it was a feast she'd laid out for us.

'I know you're not big meat eaters so I've laid on something special. Sit down. Tuck in. Eat up. Don't be waiting on me.'

She shuffled off towards the kitchen.

'Tongue kept us going something marvellous at Greenham.'

Soon as she'd gone, Pa turned off the fire and pushed up at every window like he was trying to escape.

'Painted shut.'

'What's tongue?'

Mo said, 'What it sounds like, Harry.'

Dan tasted his and liked it.

Pa pulled a zip-lock bag from out his pocket, started stuffing tongues inside.

'This isn't working is it, hun?'

Mo gave him a flat line of a smile.

It wasn't the tongue they were talking about. You could hear Granma crashing about in the kitchen.

I lifted my lettuce with my fork, see if there were creepy crawlies underneath.

Pa said, 'You don't have to eat that, Harry. I'll eat it for you.'

He seemed so sad about it that I took a bite. It was all right, actually. She'd rolled the bits of lettuce into parcels, packed with sugar.

'Dan Dan, give to Papa.'

Dan gripped his tongue in two tight fists, then held it out. Pa leaned in. Dan snatched it back. Pa crashed into the table.

'Oh shit, the Spode,' he said. 'Daniel. Please. Give it up.'

Dan giggled, lost his grip.

That tongue came at Pa so quick it licked his good shirt.

Pa said the f-word.

Dan banged the table with his fists and wailed, 'Maw Dum! Maw Dum!'

Pa stuffed the tongues into Mo's handbag just as Granma shuffled in carrying an enamel plate piled high with, oh, no . . .

'It was always your favourite, was it not, Dominic?'

After that they put her in a home.

'Do you remember Granma, Harry?'

I sat on the big bed with Pa's funeral clothes, watched him lay out his pants, tried to think of something kind to say.

Even his pants looked worn and tired.

After a bit I said, 'She was real bendy, Pa.'

He raked a hand through his hair. It was thinner than before, grey at the sides. You could see the exact shape of his skull.

'It was cruel luck, Grampy going first. He was her rock.'

Pa counted out his socks. He looked skinny and ill. You could believe it was his own funeral he was packing for. He had five pairs of socks, and added in a couple more.

'You'll be home for Christmas, won't you, Pa?'

He put out three dark ties, picked one up again, wound it tight round his hand, bulging his veins and stared like he needed to check he still had blood in them.

'Harry, I should have said. I may be gone a little longer.'

'How many effects has she got?'

'It's not about . . .' He pulled the tie tighter. It must have hurt. 'You know, I think it would help us all if your mother and I had a little break.'

'Can I go to Otis and Joan's?'

'A little break from each other, pet, a little time apart.'

'Oh.'

I knew what that meant. It happened to Piggy. A Little Time Apart led to Trial Separations and, next thing you knew, your dad lived in Balham and some man with a beard and BO was humping your mother and making you eat All Bran for breakfast.

Pa piled the pants, the socks, the ties, three suits and, I couldn't count the shirts, into the giant wheely holdall Daniel once rode around Skiathos airport, waving and smiling like a king.

'But, you can't miss Christmas, Pa.'

He threw in a couple of pairs of jeans, looked me dead in the face and said, 'Whatever happens, Harry, I will not let you down.'

Obviously, he was planning to let me down.

19

I picked up a Christmas card of snowy mountains with no people or animals and some stuff about cancer on the back. Inside it said,

'Thinking of you at this difficult time. The Dudleys.'

No mention of Pansy, Steve or Baby Greg. Was it supposed to be a secret that other people still had the right number of children tucked up and safe in their beds?

'Where's the Smarties, Mo?'

Doug Dudley was something big in Smarties, got funny-coloured ones for free. They always sent Smarties.

Mo reached across the table, nearly touched my hand.

The doorbell rang. Mo dashed out, gave the delivery man one of her new chirpy laughs. Then she zipped down the hall and up the stairs so fast I couldn't see if that box was the right size for in-line skates like I'd dropped all those hints about.

I'd made her a Celtic cross eggshell mosaic in art. Forty-six individual pieces, it took. Silvers, golds and bronze, I mixed them myself. Three coats of varnish. I'd stuck it on card, a safety pin on the back. It was big but she could wear it as a brooch if she liked.

I hadn't actually bought her anything because we'd agreed,

no decorations this year, no big fuss, but after she'd stashed I don't know how many mystery boxes in Dan's room I thought maybe I should have, you know, if she was going to all that trouble over me.

She came back, puffed and buzzing like those kids Pa says are reared on Coke and Walkers Crisps, laid into her pile of envelopes with a knife.

'The Smarties, Mo. Where are they?'

'Ah, now. You're too big for Smarties, darling.'

Bloody Dudleys. I could send their card back, put inside, 'Harry's still around, you know. He still eats chocolate.'

'You can have these if you like,' she said, pushing a black box, like a tiny coffin, across the table.

I opened it. Two silver balls – you couldn't eat them.

'Who're they from?'

'Brenda Beazley. Met her in antenatal yoga last time. Had our boys the same day. Been avoiding her ever since.' She tossed the card across the table. 'Baubles and a dog. Sweet Jesus. Must have been saving it for a suitable tragedy.'

I opened the card. The Brenda Beazley person had written, 'How are you?' with the 'are' underlined, just like people had been saying it since Daniel disappeared.

'What's with the balls?'

'They're meditation balls.' She took a long deep breath with a shiver at the end. 'Supposed to be calming.'

I rolled one round in my hand. It felt cold and it jangled. Say what you like about Shy Geoffrey and his splintery cricket bat, he kept posting fingers of fudge through the door.

Mo opened a cartoon card.

'Pah! Gordon from the *Guardian*. "When you're ready,

Gordon." Ready for what, exactly, Gordon? That's what I'd like to know.'

I spotted an envelope addressed to Harry Pickles. Joan's writing. I nabbed it, put it on my lap.

'They've invited me to the New Year bash, Harry. What do they expect? Yes, I'd love a glass of shampers. I suppose you staffers tire of it. Mwwah! Mwwah!'

She kissed the air and sloshed her coffee at me.

I had a peek inside my envelope. A note from Joan and Otis, 'All our love' and kisses, plus a plasticated card, home-made. On the front, it said, 'Otis. No Mission Impossible', with a picture of him in his firefighting gear. On the back, all his numbers and hers. They'd punched a hole in it, pushed a cord through, like I should wear it round my neck.

'You've got RSI?' Mo banged on. 'Rotten luck. Me? Ah, now . . . You heard, of course I've lost my son. Of course you did! You as good as led the paper on it! Mwwah! Mwwah! We must do lunch.'

She slammed her mug down on the table.

'Jesus, Harry! I mean for God's sake! Jesus, Harry!'

She'd be telling me next she's thirty-nine.

'Nothing from the *Mail*,' she said. 'Heartless shits.'

I decided not to tell her about my card.

'Gotcha!' Happy noises and a shiver rushed in through the window I'd opened for the pee smell in the night.

'Happy Christmas, Harry,' Biffo said.

'Same to you with knobs on.'

I got up, pulled the blind, watched Callum stalk his dad

around the frosty bushes. The pair of them were puffing steam it was so cold.

Cal took aim, fired — a real life laser, looked like.

Pchow! 'Gotcha!'

His dad clutched at his belly, rolled over, dead.

We didn't see much of Cal's dad, but Christmas Day he'd turn up with the best presents you could buy in all America. He had on a stupid duvet coat, the kind that make thin people fat, plus a shiny breastplate thing that must have known when it was hit. It said,

'Fidalidy. Fidalidy.'

I didn't want a laser gun, thank you. In-line skates would do for me. Plus, not feeling sad — my present to myself. Like Christmas Day those soldiers left their trenches to play footie with the enemy, I'd called a truce.

I padded down, heard Mo in their room on the phone.

'Oh, Dom, you know, he's so tough, he's so Brazilian.' Whatever that meant.

I searched the living room. No presents. Mo was brilliant at hiding things. Tried the kitchen, the utility room, snuck back up both flights of stairs to have a peek in Dan's room. Refused to think of Daniel crouched in ambush on the stair. No Pasaran. We're just not having it.

Dan's door was locked.

Mo, still on the phone.

'I'm family, yes, yes . . . . . . Evening, five til eight, I've got it . . . . . . Wendy Savage Ward, third floor. Lovely. Mmmm. And what about Bank holidays? . . . . . . Oh, poor you.'

I went downstairs and ate my Cheerios.

Under my bed. Of course! Why didn't I think of it

before? I ran on up. Through the window I heard Ben and Sebastiano in the bushes, having hysterics. Typical seven year olds.

Under the bed: fluff.

I heard Mo put the phone down. I grabbed the eggshell brooch, dashed in.

'Happy Christmas, Mo!'

'Oh, Harry. Christmas?' The way she put her finger to her lips, I could tell she wasn't joking.

I said, 'We are doing Christmas, aren't we?'

She tightened her mouth at me the way she did some-times on deadline days when we weren't supposed to bother her.

I hid the brooch behind my back.

'I thought this year we'd just pretend it was a normal day.'

We were so quiet for a bit it seemed Ben and Sebastiano's laughter was right there in the room with us.

A normal day? There's nothing normal about pretending Christmas isn't happening! Even the Bernsteins had lights!

'Harry, don't be like that.'

'Like what?' I hadn't said a thing.

'Harry, wait!'

I didn't hear the rest of it. I'd legged it back to my room, thrown my door shut in her face.

It wasn't right. It wasn't fair. I pulled my duvet off and stomped it on the floor. Threw my pillow at the door.

It wasn't RIGHT.

Sometimes you have to pull your socks up, get your chin up, pull yourself together. I had to keep on living, go to school and do my tests and act like I was normal. Why couldn't Mo?

I tried to tear my sheet. It wouldn't give.

Now, stealing Christmas! Wasn't FAIR.

I kicked the wall. It hurt my foot.

I looked around for something else to break. There, on the floor, my masterpiece in hand-painted wrapping paper, hand-painted by me.

And Pa! AWOL at Christmas! How long did funerals take?

I ripped the paper off and tore it at the window. A hundred tiny shreds of hand-painted wrapping paper snowed down on Ben and Sebastiano.

Sebastiano said, 'I've been in a time machine. I'm gonna whack you before you get born.'

Ben wrestled him down. 'I'll whack you first. I'll whack your mum before she humps for you.'

'I heard that,' said Sebastiano's mum.

WHO – CARES?

I had miscounted. There were forty-nine individual pieces in my Celtic cross eggshell mosaic. I got a pen and dug out every one.

It wasn't – FAIR. That life went on. It wasn't – FAIR.

What's that?

Cal, flying through my tears.

What's that?

The coolest in-line skates I'd ever seen.

He had on black elbow pads, kneepads, wrist pads.

No!

No!

No!

It wasn't – FAIR!

'Harry, I'm sorry,' Mo was saying behind the door. 'I'll make it up to you. Just you wait. Things are going to change.'

Oh, yeah.

'Weheyheyhey!' yelled Callum.

Did he have to be so loud about it? I hoped he'd fall and crack his head.

Mo's footsteps tapped back into her room.

I watched Cal spin round the corner, flip up and fly.

What a stunt! I hope it kills you.

I watched Cal's arms rotate like windmill sails, his feet rise up behind him, his body tilt, tip forward.

I heard the *thuck* that must have been his face. His body followed, then his skates.

Clatter, clatter on the concrete.

After that, he was quite still.

I watched the path turn red. For a while, four heartbeats maybe, nothing happened.

Then, I'd no idea Cal's mum could run so fast. She scrambled down beside him, barelegged in the cold. His dad charged over, still in his silly breastplate like a big fat kid. Cal's mum looked up with laser eyes – at me or Callum's dad, I couldn't tell.

Her lips said, 'Happy now?'

Seemed everyone but Cal was puffing steam.

It was days before I heard Cal wasn't dead. By then I had fresh troubles on my plate.

'Drink up your juice,' said Mo on New Year's Eve. 'I've made it specially.'

It tasted kind of bitter but I knocked it back because she'd gone to all that trouble. She took the glass, she tucked me in.

'Harry, I've an apology for you,' she said. She had on a sparkly smile, a neat black suit, and makeup.

'I've ruined Christmas for you. Sorry, darling.'

She sat on the bed, she took my hands. Her hands were damp.

'But, you know, things are going to get better. I promise you. And soon.' She kissed my head.

'Wish me luck.' She didn't say what for.

'Good luck,' I said. She tucked me in again.

'You will sleep well,' she said, which seemed to me a funny way of putting it.

We bounced over plough furrows, felt like. No give in them. Must be frozen.

I spat, blew playing cards off my face.

Tried to wedge myself, one hand on the ceiling, one on the floor, so I wouldn't get knocked about like Daniel.

Bounce! Dan flew up. Clunked his head again. His poor face, bloody.

That spade shot by. Not shiny now, splattered in mud.

The engine made a strangled whine. That man seemed to be fighting with his steering wheel.

I was thinking. Actually thinking. I could do it. The fear and something worse must have let go a bit. The something that had to be done, maybe I could do that, too, at least maybe give it a try.

Bounce! Black bin bags rustled, flew about. An icy breeze sped through the door. Open! Just a crack but I could kick it.

Bounce! Daniel tumbled my way. I grabbed his wrist. Kick,

kick, kicked the door. One more kick — it might just give.

I snapped awake.

Mo shifted in and out of focus. Dan's fingers slipped through mine.

I tried to lift my head. A cold, steel, jangling ball rolled about inside it. Daylight filled the room but it was night-time only seconds ago. Mo's lips moved. Her eyes were wide and glad. My tongue felt fat.

'Darling,' she said. 'Terrific news!'

A new arrival

A new arrival

20

'What? What do you mean?'

'We've had a baby, Harry! You've got a little brother!' She sat down on my bed.

'But, Mo, how come?'

'You know all that!'

'I know, I just . . .' I pushed up. God, my head hurt. 'I never even guessed.'

'We didn't want to worry you.'

'Pa knows?'

'Of course Pa knows.' She checked her nails. 'He thinks it's grand.'

He should be here.

'What about the bump?'

'The bump?'

'Where was the bump?'

'Oh, Harry, third babies, sometimes they don't show at all.'

'Oh.'

She touched her tummy.

'Of course I had a bump. Perhaps you didn't notice it.'

'But, Mo, I just don't get it.'

'Harry . . .' The way she said it I knew I'd gone too far.

'Harry, good things happen sometimes to make up for the bad things that happen. Please don't spoil *this* for us.'

As if losing Daniel for them wasn't enough.

I tried to think of something nice to say, put things right. God, my head hurt.

'You've been ovulating, haven't you, Mo?'

Her nearly black eyebrows met in the middle.

'That's the usual way.'

'Why didn't you wake me? I could have said Push or something.'

She seemed to relax a bit.

'Harry, I'm an old hand.'

It didn't fit. I didn't get it. She must be making it up. Then I heard crying. There really was a baby. She whisked off to do something to it.

Mo brought the baby in.

A real, live baby with a baby smell and everything.

It wasn't right. It didn't fit.

'Look at you,' Mo told him. 'Look at you.'

She smiled a real Mo smile. My Mo, the happy Mo.

It wasn't right. It didn't fit, but here was something I could do.

'Look at you.'

For Mo.

Believe. Only believe. It didn't seem so much to ask for losing Daniel.

Clouds moved and happy yellow light lit up my room.

Believing wasn't so very difficult. I believed I might one day invent a new technique for growing bones inside people.

Or break a world sprint record. Maybe do the record first, and then the orthopaedic stuff. I half believed some people could beam themselves into other places if they could only think hard enough. Believing Dan was dead and gone and never coming back, that was hard. But this?

I said, 'Hey, Mo, can I hold him?'

Things change.

Baby wakes and feeds and sleeps and wakes. He's put some beat into our lives.

I call him Little Boy. He snuggles into me. I'm really good at holding him. And feeding him. I'd change him too, if it was only pee, but Mo says, that's all right.

Mo sings.

He belches louder than you'd think.

If I dream I dream of things I don't remember in the morning. No car. No motorway. No muddy spade. My bed stays dry. The itch itch itching for something to do. It's gone. I've got something to do. I can believe.

We don't go out. The doorbell rings. We hold our breath and wait for them to go. The phone rings and we let it.

His eyelashes come. Not even lines like mine, no. Clumps of them.

Sometimes I feel his poo's vibrations through his nappy like a rocket taking off.

He smiles at me.

He smiles.

At me.

*   *   *

Day by day I build a wall, true stories reinforced with kryptonite, a wall to keep the questions out, keep Mo and Little
Boy safe inside.

Take that family Otis's mum told us all about the Carnival before.

Flipping chicken on the grill, she was. Us lazing in her
deck chairs. Sizzle and spit. Ooh, those plantains smelt
good.

'I want burgers for my tea, he sez.

Boo hoo, she sez.

Burgers, he sez.

I'll get em myself, he sez.

Opens the freeze-box.

What's this in here? he sez. A leg of PORK? he sez. You
think I'm MADE of money? It moved! What? What? My
GOD, woman! THIS HERE'S MY SON!'

She wiped her eyes, crying, laughing or the barbecue
smoke itching her.

'Gives the boy the kiss of life! There and then on the
refrigerator cabinet! Big strong feller, now, they say. Not so
good at arithmetic. Plantain anyone?'

Things often aren't how they're supposed to be. It's almost
normal to be weird.

Like Cal's mum, with Cal's new baby, the day Cal's dad
moved down to Brighton with That Woman.

'You look terrific, really strong,' said Mo, when Cal's mum,
called Felicia, opened the door.

She looked like death. There was sick on her jumper.

She took us to an upstairs room that smelt of cigarettes
and poo.

I nudged Dan so he'd see the giant pair of paper pants

she had hanging off the wardrobe door – blood on them. Dan made his yuck face. I expect that was the wardrobe Cal said she bought from Elephant Antiques to drive his dad completely ape. I don't know how that worked exactly but it did.

She had a Moses basket. At one end was a baby, seriously ugly. At the other end, a kangaroo, head down, bum in the air like it couldn't bear looking at the baby.

I didn't laugh on account of me and Mo had only just been having a mature discussion about tact.

'Poor you, Felicia,' I was going to say, but I wasn't completely sure about it.

Mo said, 'Ah.' Just that.

A tube train trundled by. *D'dee D'dee.*

Cal's mum made a cough, like she was waiting for someone to say something nice about her baby.

Dan got busy sorting out the kangaroo.

At last Mo said, 'Persephone. Such a . . . melodious name.'

'The one thing we agree on,' said Felicia. 'We thought about Penelope, but Penny's so coarse.'

'I see,' said Mo.

Her cousin who got hit by a truck was called Penny.

'Persephone, though. You can't ruin Persephone.'

They'd murder her if she went to our school.

Dan got the kangaroo right way up, tucked it in with the baby and said,

'There you go, Spuffy.'

Felicia's jaw tightened. My lips twitched. A snort popped out.

'Oh God, the pollen,' said Mo, with a big-trouble-coming

look that helped me get a hold on myself. 'He needs his medication. Right away. We'll see ourselves out.'

Cal's mum said goodbye from the landing, touched her baggy tummy and said,

'Can you believe it? A whole extra person in there?'

I could easily believe it.

(I ought to tell you, Spuffy – Little P, we called her – turned out all right and not ugly after all.)

And what about Jesus? All over the world, people getting excited over a baby whose mum hadn't even humped for it.

All the same . . .

As days go by I feel the furniture move in on me. Walls slide. Ceilings sink like in the Batman comics. I catch her in the kitchen doing that eyes closed sitting still thing, only rocking a bit. One hand holding the other, her bit-down nails kind of digging in. The air gets thin. The tasty treats Mo makes stick to my mouth. I need to get outside and breathe.

21

Miss Bliss broke off, her eyes flicked over me, a look and then another one – 'Harry, on my desk, a tiny gift to welcome you all back' – then carried on.

You'd think she'd trip and hurt herself, walking round the room like that, reading aloud. But she stepped over people's bags and stuff like she had a radar tracking system hid inside her creaky knees.

On her desk, a bowl with olives in it, oily and dimpled, the same shining deep purply-brown, almost black, of her eyes. I took one. It was my first Christmas present, unless you counted Brenda Beazley's meditation balls, which I didn't. I tucked myself into my desk. The lads nodded hello and got their heads down quick.

I slipped the olive into my mouth, sucked on its sweet, salty flesh, tore it, pushed out the stone, munched and swallowed, licked my fingers, wished I could eat ten more right now this minute I was so hungry.

Piggy hissed, 'You OK, Picks?'

'Triffic, thanks.'

He looked at me kind of nosy. Same look Mr Donald gave me when I ran into him at the gates and he said, 'Pickles, just the man I want to . . .' Only I didn't hear the rest of it cos I was running for the building.

Maybe I looked worried on account of the big trouble I'd be in when Mo found out I wasn't in the house. I tried to look normal, get a grip on the story Miss Bliss was reading about a little boy's first day at school.

Piggy hissed, 'Wodjoo get, Picks?'

I mustn't blurt about the baby.

'Harry. Wodjoo get?'

Across the room — God knows how she heard him, we reckoned she had every table bugged — Miss Bliss gave Piggy her 'you've been warned' face and had another funny look at me, like I had my jumper inside out or had forgot to zip my flies. I checked. It wasn't that.

That boy's sisters wrapped him up in scarves and stuffed a baked potato in his pocket. Dan liked baked potatoes. The room went dark and light again. My hands felt wet. My bum felt full, you know, like I might poo a noisy wet one. That little boy's potato burned his thigh.

Peter and Terry, playing battleships, gave me a funny look when they thought I couldn't see them. I checked my nose for bogies hanging out.

The ceiling cracked and twisted. Kids carried on like always, doodling, staring out the window, passing notes.

Someone stole that boy's potato.

It wasn't right.

Kids carried on like they had no idea the air was getting sucked out of the room.

It wasn't right the way Mo called our baby Dan Dan. It wasn't right the way we kept him as our secret. It wasn't right, that sad-happy-sad-again flip she did. You know, one minute loving Little Boy and laughing. Next minute looking like he'd never come along. It wasn't right — but it was better than before.

The room flashed bright and dark. The Hoberman sphere crashed down and bounced from desk to desk, and no-one saw.

A stumpy girl came up to that little boy. She had springy hair. He had a stick in his hand. He hit her on the head with his stick.

A spluttery cough came out of me.

Miss Bliss said, 'Harry, are you unwell?'

I made out I had a frog in my throat, but it wasn't that.

I was the Dutch boy with his finger in the dyke, not just the boy, the dyke as well, and any minute a sea of tears might burst out of me and flood the whole wide world.

That boy who hit the girl said the policeman's hand on the shoulder always comes as a surprise. Miss Bliss looked my way. Like it was a sign or something. All the stories that she could have picked and she picked that one. I twisted in my seat. My mouth went dry. Was this how Granma felt when she went bonkers, all mixed up?

A sharp knock at the door. I had to squeeze my bum-hole shut.

'A little word, Miss Balisciano?'

Our school secretary, Miss Fink, did her special whisper that might come in handy one day if the school was burning down and Mr Donald had lost his megaphone.

She hissed 'Harry Pickles' every other word, sent dagger looks in my direction. Everyone had a stare at me.

'Harry, Mr Donald would like to see you. Please follow Mrs Finkelstein.' Miss Bliss smiled.

'Be cool,' said Biffo.

I was cool.

I knew exactly what was happening. Like Miss Fink's

bristly whisper had scrubbed my head out. It was obvious.

I started gathering my things.

Miss Bliss said, 'Don't worry, Harry, you won't be needing those.'

Of course. They'd be no use where I was going.

At the door I had one last look around the classroom. Who would visit me? Brian Smith shot me the panda look he'd had since the operation on his septum that got bent in footie. Pete and Terry, heads together, argued over whether tanks could take out submarines. Piggy smiled, gave me his thumbs up.

'No dawdling, please.'

Miss Fink clacked down the corridor in her grey skirt and cardigan like she was getting me used to how things would be from now on.

The bell rang for break.

There'd be lots of bells where I was going.

Would there be breaking rocks for punishments? It might help, you know, help make me feel less bad about not checking that Dan was on the bus.

Chairs scraped.

Maybe there'd be football. With a change of air and venue I might regain my form.

Doors opened, noisy kids spilled out.

Would they take me straightaway? But it was chicken stroganoff for lunch.

The corridor walls moved in on me. Darkness gathered round my head. Somehow I knew I had to check on Mo and Little Boy before they took me off to prison.

'I need the toilet something awful, Miss.'

'The senior boys' is just here, Harry.'

'It's blocked. I gotta go outside.'

I legged it past the bogs and through the gates and up the road. The cold pinched at my nipples – I'd left my parka in the cloakroom. The ground was hard and slippery. I didn't care. I ran and ran and halfway home all I could hear was Miss Fink megaphoning after me.

22

You could see through the hole that hadn't been there before that the kitchen wall was hollow.

I ran my fingers round the edge. What had made it? A fist, or a boot, a hammer maybe.

Something crunched under my feet.

I looked about me.

Chairs upended. Bits of glass and crockery everywhere. Sugar. Flour. Pasta. Cheerios. A twisted something. Maybe the coffee grinder.

Like some kind of nutcase had gone completely bonkers in our kitchen.

It didn't take me long to work it out. The man. He'd come to get the rest of us. Complete his set.

Little Boy howled. And I realised he'd been howling for a long while.

23

Little Boy sat bolt upright on his bed. Screaming. His mouth filled the whole of his face. A fat worm of vein throbbed in his temple. Could babies' heads explode?

'It's all right, Little Boy. It's OK. I'll fetch Mo for you.'

I legged it down the stairs, swung into Mo's room.

'Mo. Wake up. The baby's crying.'

I shook her shoulder. Her hand flopped off her chest onto the bed. The fingers had little cuts on them, like she'd tried clearing up that broken glass and stuff.

'Please. Come on. Get up.'

The ceiling trembled, Little Boy screamed so loud.

I raced upstairs, sat on his bed, caught my breath, reached over, stroked his face, tried to speak softly, sound calm.

'It's aaallright.'

I hauled him across the bed, picked him up and held him close.

'Come on, Little Boy. Saaaaallright.'

His mouth next to my ear like that I couldn't think for noise.

I stood up and tried the hip-swaying thing.

It made him angrier and hurt my knees.

Jesus, he was heavy.

'Now, stop it!'

He wouldn't stop it.

I sat down.

Sometimes you've got to be firm. You've got to give them clear boundaries.

'Little Boy, listen to Harry.'

He was so loud I couldn't see straight.

'STOP IT LITTLE BOY!'

That stopped him.

Then he started up again, only louder than before.

So I shook him.

Just a little bit, not the way you're not supposed to. I only wanted him to stop it.

He wouldn't stop it. My whole body clenched.

I felt scared. Not of the man. Scared of me. What I would do.

'Stay calm,' said Biffo.

All right for him to say.

'Breathe easy. Think it through. If it aint hunger, it's wind. If it aint wind, the boy's lonely an if he aint lonely . . . well, it's the hot chocolate sauce.'

I took a long breath, felt it cool me.

I made two decisions.

Not to shake him again.

No way on earth was I touching his poo.

'I'm here, Little Boy. Harry's here. It's all right, now.'

I spoke slowly, softly.

It worked like the volume control.

His sobbing calmed.

His body softened.

Then he jammed his foot into my balls, let out a shriek that hurt my teeth.

'Guess we can eliminate lonely, Kid.'

I didn't shake him.

There was a bottle propped against the pillow. I picked it up, aimed the teat at Little Boy's angry mouth, saw my chance and moved in quick.

A nasty backfist bashed the bottle from my hand and landed hard against my eye. I ground my teeth.

'You're doing great. So. He aint hungry. Now, take your pick. Wind? Or the chocolaty stuff.'

I stood and heaved him up against my shoulder. Patted his back.

'Burp.'

He wouldn't burp. He screamed. His breath burned my ear. A strange spangly feeling took hold of the whole of my head.

I didn't shake him.

I lay him on the bed, then stood up, pressed my face against the wall where it felt nice and cool. Had a think.

Two thoughts popped up.

In olden days when ladies got hysterical gentlemen slapped them.

Pillows are good at muffling noise.

Just for a minute. Give me a breather. I wasn't going to hurt him. What else could I do? Mo wouldn't wake up and I was only a boy.

'Snap out of it, Kiddo! Guy like you knows what needs doing. Just do it.'

Like they say in the ads.

I took a closer look at Little Boy. He had on a yellow

bodysuit thing I didn't understand. He must have been sewn into it. There was no way out.

'Frisk him.'

He didn't want to be frisked. Bubbles inflated from his nostrils, exploded in his face. My ears buzzed like that time Fergus McNally kicked me in the head.

'Keep frisking.'

All the way down his back, under his bum, that's where I found the poppers.

I peeled him like a banana, found the nappy straight-away.

I was planning my approach when Little Boy stopped crying.

I spotted tissues and Pampers by the hamster cage.

Things were looking up.

I got my hearing back.

'Ughuh . . . Ughuh,' said Little Boy.

It didn't sound right. He might have swallowed his tongue. I leaned in close.

He scratched my eyes with sharp, deadly claws, let rip another earbleeding yell. Blinded, I jerked away, made a fist and pulled it back.

'We were thinking about the nappy, Kid. Relax and count to ten.'

I'd got to nine before I had my brilliant idea. The thing to do was treat the nappy like pants. Pants I knew about.

I tried to pull them down.

They wouldn't come.

Across the front, at the top, pink and purple teddy bears played trumpets and laughed like it was some kind of joke.

That's where I saw two bits of sticky tape. I pulled them. Everything loosened.

It might be ugly. I'd better count myself in.

Three.

'I'll betcha it's not as bad as you're thinking.'

Two.

I leaned back.

One.

I pulled the nappy down.

Blast Off!

Great slimy landslides oozed across the duvet. The stink had me gagging. I grabbed for tissues. I turned back and Little Boy was squelching his poo in two tight little fists. I started mopping but, can you believe it, Little Boy's bumhole opened up like the cave in the Thunderbirds. Out came more poo.

'Stay calm, Kid. Could be worse.'

That's when he peed in my face. It stung like nettles where he'd scratched me. But I had something else to think about. Something was badly wrong. Down there, in his private place. A great big wound where Little Boy's penis ought to be.

No wonder he'd been screaming.

I tried to work it out. It didn't take long. The man had broken in, trashed the kitchen, banjaxed Mo and scarpered with Little Boy's penis.

My tears broke. Strong, gulping sobs that made everything wobbly. I mopped up Little Boy, put a nappy on him, couldn't figure out how the sticky bits worked so I got some pants from Dan's drawer, pulled them over the top. He looked like Superman.

209

I tried wiping his hands but there were too many tiny bits to them. I got the duvet out from under him, tossed the dirty things inside, wiped my hands and threw it on the floor. What did it matter? It was only a duvet and Little Boy's penis had gone.

I picked up the bottle, put it on the bed, found Dan's dressing gown, wrapped Little Boy, gathered him up and held him close. I didn't mind about the noise, now, or the stink. The hip-swaying thing came easier now I understood why he was angry. Poor Little Boy.

'It's all right. It's all right,' I said and it calmed me.

His sobbing sank into low humming noises. He seemed to be singing. I hummed along, fell in with his song, sat down on the bed. He took a little milk, grew soft in my arms. His head lolled on my shoulder. The teat fell away. He burped, warm and wet. I put him down and he stirred. I put my hand on his chest, said,

'It's all right, Little Boy. It's all right. You can stay sleeping.' And he did.

Mo lay in the exact same position as when I had left her. I touched her hand. Cold and too still. Mine was hot and shaking. Her skin was kind of grey, her lips were blue, but it was the coldness that scared me. Grampy in his coffin.

I saw everything like in a film, like from one corner of the ceiling. A boy in school uniform standing up straight, looking down at his mother. Not daring to think one specially scary thing. Had to do something, fast. Didn't know what. He'd seen drawings of mouth-to-mouth. Him and his friends had laughed.

He shifted his weight from one foot to the other, put his hands in his pockets, took them out, folded his arms behind his back, unfolded them, reached over, put one hand on his mother where her heart ought to be. Was it supposed to feel that way? He felt his own. Jack-hammer. Through his jumper, under his school shirt, he ran his finger along the hard, straight edge of Otis's card.

24

Men's voices on the stairs below us . . .

'Easy on the turn.'

'Tilt it.'

Grunts, like they were shifting a piano.

'Nice looking baby. What seems to be the trouble, mate?'

How could he be so cool about it?

'Otis.'

My finger jerked about so much it was difficult to point.

'The man took his penis.'

Saying it felt dangerous, made it real.

He dropped to his haunches alongside my brother. Opened the dressing gown.

'I couldn't work the sticky bits.'

'Pants your idea? Good thinking, mate. Snug as a bug.'

Otis slid the pants down, off the ends of Little Boy's feet. He passed me the pants.

The baby slept on.

I gripped my thumbs in my fists, got ready for Otis's shock.

There was shuffling on the landing. I grabbed Otis's arm.

'It's OK, Harry. Just a friend of mine.' He turned his

head towards the door and whispered, 'Hush a minute.'

'We've got to talk.' It was a woman, frightened.

'Harry, will you excuse me?' Otis said, as if I was a grown-up.

He tiptoed out onto the landing. I watched Little Boy, his lips kissing together like he was sucking at a titty.

The voice said tightly, 'Otis, this is so not according to procedure.'

'Karen. My boy is not going to be handled according to procedure.'

'I have to call this in.'

'You do what you have to, Kaz.'

I caught a flash of someone. A policeman, all in uniform, cuffs and everything, only he was a she and blonde and kind of gorgeous.

'Otis, this isn't . . . This could –'

'Lose you your promotion?'

'That isn't fair.'

'Karen. None of this is fair. Five minutes. Please. It's all I ask. I'll never ask you anything again.'

There was a sigh, more shuffling, then she tiptoed down the stairs.

Otis came in, sat down, and slowly, gently, undid the front of the nappy.

Poor Little Boy. Poor thing.

Otis didn't blink.

'Tell me what you see, mate.'

'It's a wound.'

'Is it bleeding?'

I checked. 'No, it's not.'

'Wounds bleed, mate. This is not a wound.'

He put back the nappy, sticky bits and all, held out his hand for the pants as if that was the end of it.

I wouldn't give him the pants.

'It's not there,' I croaked. 'His penis is gone.'

'Did you see it? Did you ever see it, mate?'

If you can picture the calmest thing in your memory. Calm. Calm. Well, double it and Otis was two hundred times calmer than that.

'Mo wouldn't let me in the bathroom,' said my voice.

Me, I was back in the time Otis helped make a birthday cake for Joan. Dan greased the tins. I sieved the flour and the sugar, cracked the eggs, all the important things, the stirring, the pouring, didn't spill any, hardly. Otis wet the knife and spread the icing, squeezed pink spindly letters from the bag.

'You didn't see his penis, did you, mate?'

He must have taken the pants from me – he was slipping the leg-holes over Little Boy's feet. A big man doing the fiddly bits.

'But, Otis. He's a BOY!'

He made a little O with his lips, put his finger there to shush me, pulled the pants up.

'How do you know he's a boy, mate?'

I heard men's voices, doors slam, something like a tank went roaring off – and sirens. They wouldn't bother with the sirens if someone was dead already. Would they?

Far away inside my head I heard a creaking, breaking, crumbling, a great big wall, it sounded like, cracking under the strain.

'Take a pew,' said Otis, budging up the bed.

We sat down, our backs to Little Boy.

'Harry,' said Otis. His eyes held onto mine. 'Harry. I'm going to tell you something. It's very hard to take. But you can handle it. You're strong, mate. Are you ready?'

I wasn't strong. I wasn't ready.

That voice came from the landing, like a wire that's going to snap.

'Otis, I've called it in. The team will be here any minute. I can't –'

'That's all I need,' said Otis, not taking his eyes off me for a second. 'Harry. Mo didn't have a little boy.'

He waited for the penny to drop.

And then it did.

'But, that's OK. It's all right if Little Boy's not a boy.'

'She didn't have a baby, Harry.'

'Girls can be cool.'

'Harry. Listen to me. Mo Didn't Have A Baby. This Baby Isn't Mo's.'

After all I'd been through to believe, if all that was a lie, we were finished. There was no coming back.

'This – Baby – Is – Another – Lady's – Baby,' he said like he was trying to get through to someone who didn't speak English.

Kryptonite blocks slipped, slid about.

'You're lying, Otis.'

'I'm not a liar, Harry.'

I watched the blood drain from my fists, my knuckles pale. I couldn't look at Otis.

'Mo didn't have a baby, Harry, not a baby of her own. She took a baby, mate. She got very ill and took one.'

Teardrops splashed up from the floor. My wall came crashing down.

'Tell me, mate. Why do you call him Little Boy?'

'He's big.'

'He's very big. Well spotted, mate. He's not a new-born, Harry. This little girl is five months old.'

'Otis, please,' that lady said.

He stared at his fingernails. Clean, always. Looked back at me all of a sudden.

'Yeah? Tell me what you're thinking.'

'Little Boy can sit up.'

'Good man. And we both know that new-borns don't. Spot on there, mate.'

Cars pulled up, doors slammed. That lady ran back up the stairs and did a kind of shouting whisper: 'Otis, I can't give you any longer.'

He stared at his hands like he was deaf. That lady huffed and puffed and scooted down the stairs.

'Anything else you was right about?'

Mo didn't feed him with her titties. Mo never let me see him naked. Mo's tummy wasn't big enough. Loads of things.

Hot tears spilled out of me. My nose ran.

'I want my Pa.'

'We'll see him later, Harry. He's at the hospital by now.'

He gave me his hanky and I blew. He watched me, steadily, like he was trying to guess my weight. Our doorbell rang, the lady let them in. I heard voices in our kitchen.

The lady dashed back up and whispered, 'Otis! Hurry, Otis! Now!'

'She's going to be all right. Mo. Isn't she, Otis?'

His eyes flicked to Daniel's bedside table.

'She's in good hands.'

I did more blowing.

'Pa got there quick.'

'It isn't far to Paddington.'

''Tis from Newcastle, Otis. You should try it.'

Otis glared at Bang Bang's empty cage. Heavy footsteps started up the stairs.

'He's been down south a while, mate.'

'But.'

'Otis, I'm really under pressure here,' the lady said.

He looked at me, his brown eyes soft and sad.

'That's a father and son chat you've got coming.'

I blubbed, 'It's all secrets, Otis.'

'Right again there, Harry. This isn't our baby.' That's when his tears came. 'This is another family's baby.'

I did an elephant roar into his hanky. He gave my leg a squeeze and sniffed and said, 'There's someone waiting downstairs for the baby.'

That lady on the landing sighed a sigh so big it might have blown the roof off.

'But no-one gave us Daniel back!'

'No-one did and that was evil, Harry.'

'Well, then.'

He opened his hands to me.

'But we're the good guys, Harry. You and me, mate. We're the good guys.'

25

I hit eject.

'It's mangled another one, Otis.'

He said, 'I hate this car.'

His elbow jammed against the window. The steering wheel scraped his knees. He was mad to sell his precious Alfa. It wouldn't solve his problem. If I'd been a policeman I'd have pulled him over in Joan's Nissan. It obviously didn't belong to him. It was crap. We were only going up the hill past Holland Park and it was grumbling.

'You never did get to tell me about that mission of yours.'

One of those sad-faced Asian nannies, tiny woman, pushed a giant white kid in a buggy up the icy pavement.

'Harry, I'm talking to you.'

Mo told me once they'd left their kids in Wakkatoo or somewhere.

'I'd like to hear about the mission.' His fireman voice.

My pledge. On pain of death. It was probably nice and warm in Wakkatoo.

'Harry!'

What did it matter? The SAS could come and kill me if they wanted. I wouldn't mind, if they were quick about it.

I spilled the beans, all the stuff about the man and the shed and the petrol and the knife and the nearly-stabbing at the Carnival. Everything.

Otis pulled up outside the surgery.

'Jesus, Harry!'

Two tears rolled down his face. I bet which one would drop off first. Left, definitely. The right one started gaining.

'Jesus!'

Probably the left would have made a late surge only Otis wiped his face.

'Number one. We have no reason, Harry, no reason at all, to think the bus driver did anything to Daniel.'

'The police thought he did.'

'Negative, Harry,' like he was on *Star Trek*. 'Negative. The police arksed you about him. The police might have arksed about me or about Dom or about the man in the moon, Harry. Police arksing don't mean nobody's guilty.'

Otis was not calm.

'I know that now, it's just –'

'Point number two. Number two, Harry.'

White foamy stuff gathered in the corners of his mouth.

'Number two, we don't know who the geeza woz you tried to stab. You nearly stabbed, for Christ sake.'

He was not calm at all. Probably been drinking too much coffee. He was always telling me it affected your mood.

'I didn't actually –'

'Jesus, Harry! And point number four. Number four, Harry. Remembering, like we agreed –'

He was spitting. And he'd missed out his point number three.

'We're the good guys. We don't set fires. In case you've forgotten, mate, I put fires out. Imagine if you'd burned the shed and the man.'

I'd imagined it.

'What if you got the wrong man?'

'But, Otis, we had loads of –'

'What if you got the right man? Jesus, Harry!'

'That would be all right, Otis.'

'It would not be all right.' He squeaked, like a big kid, his voice breaking again.

'It would be all right if he took Daniel.'

'Harry, listen to me! You do not have an idea in your head if he took Daniel. All you know is he looks a bit like the man who drove the bus who the police arksed a few questions about.'

'But if I did know he hurt Daniel, it would be all right then, Otis.'

What happened next was Otis turned so mad his face swelled up. I thought he was going to scream at me, hit me, even. But he kept both hands gripped to the wheel and when he did speak I had to slow my breathing down to hear him.

'If we knew, for sure, for dead set certain, we had the man who hurt Daniel, then you, Harry, you, my son, would have to get in line. It's a man's job, Harry. And you are not a man. You have no business, Harry, thinking these thoughts. If we knew it was him, if we really knew, then I would deal with it.'

Of course, Otis could do the killing! He'd be much better at it.

'And even then, even then, Harry, it would not be all right.'

'What? Why not?'

'It just wouldn't. Look, I'm argued out, mate. It just wouldn't. Please.'

His lips began to tremble. He held both hands up to his face, threw back his head, let out a loud, long roar.

He seemed a bit calmer after that.

'You know that someone would have called the fire brigade. I could have gone there, mate. I could have got hurt.'

I hadn't thought of that.

We stared out through the darkening windscreen at a council skip with nothing in it.

He said, 'Well, here we are.'

'Pa's here?'

'He's been staying at a flat above the surgery.'

'I never knew about a flat.'

'The locums use it.'

'Has he got a locum up there now?'

He stared hard at the skip and said, 'Far as I know he's got no-one up there, Harry.'

'Pa shouldn't have a flat.'

Otis said nothing.

'Jesus, Otis!'

'Less of your blasphemy, Harry.'

'I'm not going up there.'

He said, 'No reason why you should, mate,' then he fired up the engine and drove me back to his and Joan's like he really did hate that car.

Can we fix it?

26

'Harry, I don't want to hear that again.'

'But, Pa. Everyone calls it a loony bin.'

He'd stalled it. Always was crap at parking, even before, you know. That's why we'd gone in Doctors Only. There wasn't a space big enough in Visitors.

'Name *everyone*.'

He started the engine. Let go the handbrake. Blinked into the mirror. We jerked backwards, Pa muscling the steering wheel one way then the other.

'Kylie Kelly.'

'Since when did you care what that silly girl thought?'

'Since Mo's been in the . . . here, Pa.'

He poked round with the gear stick, we edged forwards, he softened his voice a bit.

'Harry, honey, it's a special psychiatric unit and there's no shame in that.'

Oh, yeah, brilliant. That's what I'd tell them.

He yanked at the handbrake, shoved the gear stick about.

'Nutters, Pa,'

Crrrrunch went the gears.

'I'm warning you, Harry.'

'I was only saying, that's another thing they say.'

'They should know better.' He found reverse, seemed to be doing all right.

'Sickos.'

The car jerked back, there was a soft, crumpling sound. Pa said, 'Shit!'

'Shit, shit, shit,' he said when we got out and saw what we'd hit.

It was one of mine and Otis's favourite new models, actually, a silver Porsche 968 Cabriolet convertible. Did a hundred and fifty-six miles an hour.

Pa screwed up his face like he was trying to copy the crumpled, crinkled mess we'd made of it. He should have got mad at me, seemed too tired to bother. I noticed his eyebrows. They'd gone completely grey.

'No-one seen us. We could scarper.'

'Saw us, not seen us, Harry.' He got out his notebook, scribbled a note, tore it off, stuck it under the wiper. Then he said in that sarky way he had lately, 'Bet he didn't get that on his NHS salary.'

I sat on my hand for a bit, rubbed my nose, nice and casual, check that pee stink wasn't me.

Pa took a magazine from the rack.

'These places always smell this way, honey.'

It wasn't just the stink. In that room behind the screen, the Wreck Room they called it, sad-faced people sat round in creepy armchairs watching *Bob the Builder* on the telly. Down the corridor, an old lady clanked her Zimmer frame towards us. Had on the kind of party dress that ladies wore in olden days, grey frizzy hair and bright red lipstick. She'd done her Zimmer frame up with Tinsel.

'That Biscuit is Too Big to Fit on This Plate,' said a panicky voice from the Wreck Room.

A calm lady said, 'Now, don't be silly, Charlie, it's only custard creams.'

That Zimmer lady got closer to us, scraping her frame against the wall.

'I Must Insist,' wailed the biscuit man. 'Can't You See? Are You Completely Mad? It Will Not Fit I Tell You.'

'Pa. Were they like this before they came here?'

He looked up from his magazine – it was called *Practical Caravan* – he put his finger to his white dry lips and whispered, 'Later, Harry.'

The calm lady said, 'There, Charlie. Like I told you. One custard cream. No problem.'

The Zimmer lady crashed her frame against the waiting room doorway. It wouldn't fit, it was obvious.

'It Will Not Fit,' wailed the biscuit man. 'That Plate Will Never Fit On This Table. Take It Away. Or I Will Call the Authorities.'

'Charlie, love, we are the authorities. Now, come on, you're upsetting Alphonse.'

'I'm Not Upset. I'm Not Upset.'

My lips twitched.

I never knew Pa was so interested in caravans.

The Zimmer lady backed up a bit, got steady, then threw herself at the doorway.

Someone turned up the telly. We got a blast of 'Bob the builder. Can we fix it? Bob the builder. Yes we can!'

I clenched my teeth and started running through my all-time favourite Spurs team.

I'd got to substitutes before a black lady with a bunch of keys clipped to her jeans ran up and helped the Zimmer lady do a turn.

'Tea-time now, Louise. You like your tea, love.'

They'd best not talk to Mo like that. She'd give them what for.

Out of nowhere, a beardy nutcase dashed in, grabbed Pa's hand and yanked him to his feet. He had on cords, a woolly jumper with a pen stuck in it, a tartan Swatch watch and a permanent stuck-on grin. I looked about me for the panic button.

Pa said, 'Harry, this is Dr Fartyson.' That's what it sounded like. 'He's been looking after Mo.'

I nearly choked.

'Harry!' said Dr Fartyson. 'We meet at last!'

He pumped my arm. It really hurt.

'Don't be nervous, Harry. I'm here to help.'

He took us down corridor after corridor, narrower every time, past people I couldn't tell were doctors, visitors or nutters. Outside one door he stopped and knocked. He threw the door open and sang out,

'Mo-oh! Visit-ors!'

As if she was the kind of person you could burst in on like a moron.

Tan, teeth and big lips grinned up at us til Mo put down *Hello* magazine. A weak smile touched her lips, white, dry, papery like Pa's. On her wrist she had a small pink plaster. I expect that's where they had to stick the drip in.

I went to kiss her. She smelled of hospital. Pa kissed her too, a peck. When he put his hand on top of hers I heard the sound of sugar paper rubbed against itself.

'How's school?' she said.

I could have told her about the Venn diagrams, about how we had to choose a coloured sash and stand in groups and get drawn round, and Peter and Terry got in the same group like always now, and I got in no group at all. And we had to think of examples of what to 'describe' with a Venn diagram. And Adrian Mahoney said, people who like Chelsea, Miss, and people who like Arsenal, and My Sissay said, people who had brothers and people who had sisters, and Brian Smith said, Yeah, Miss, and people with no brothers and sisters could stand on the outside, there, Miss, and his finger landed just where I was standing, and there was a kind of group holding of breath like the world had stopped for a minute, and the whole entire class got a simultaneous attack of embarrassment, and Kylie Kelly looked at me and chewed her tongue and scratched her impetigo, because even she got it, even she understood that that's where I was now, and didn't everyone know it, that's where I was more than ever now my mum had stole a baby, on the outside.

Pa said, 'Your mother's asking you a question.'

I said, 'I get to go to the pizza party Tuesday, Mo,' which wasn't true.

'Good man,' she said.

Pa said, 'How's the medication?'

She said, 'My mouth feels dry all the time.'

'Splendid!' said Dr Fartyson, backing off towards the door. 'We'll soon have her up and about in the Wreck Room.'

'She's not a wreck!' I would have said only I didn't want to make things worse for her.

Dr Fartyson flashed that stupid grin, chucked me under the chin like I was five and said,

'My first name's Bob. You know what that means, don't you, Harry?'

I had no idea.

'Can we fix her? Yes we can!'

I could have puked.

Mo and Pa had one of those deadly boring grown-up chats about people in the square and at the surgery, and who was moving jobs or moving house and other stuff that helped fill up the long, grey gap before we were allowed to go home.

Pa needed a pee on the way out. I waited by the nurses' station so I'd be safe from nutters, watched Dr Fartyson getting steamed up on the phone.

'I am not having a good day, Samantha, thank you very much. Some cretin's pranged my fucking Porsche.'

That annoying grin had completely vanished from his face.

27

I promised Pa I wouldn't say loony bin any more.

Here's what happened those months that Mo was in the mad house. We kept the house clean and the fridge filled and we ate fresh fruit every day. We got my homework done and the washing washed, which was handy because my car dreams had come screeching back. Most nights we trained like we had the big fight coming. Otis dropped in now and then to keep us on our toes.

'You need to do some bag work, mate.'

Pa said, 'Otis, please, I'm all done in.'

I kept on skipping. *Tap-tap. Tap-tap.* The boxer's way. Right, right. Left, left.

'Take it from me, Dom. You need some bag work.'

'Otis, I haven't got it in me.'

Couldn't he see Pa was skinny and ill like Fag Ash Phil at the newspaper kiosk? And those guys from the Aids place. Skeleton. Thin yellow skin just about holding it together.

Tap-tap. Tap-tap.

Skipping's cool. Helps you go numb in the head.

'You don't know what you've got in you, mate, til it comes out. The bag. Two minutes. Starting, now.'

Otis clicked the stopwatch.

Serve him right if Pa keeled over dead.

Pa got his hands up, got his legs into position. Can you believe he still had to watch his feet? Eyed the bag then hit it.

Flump.

'Focus. Focus, Dom. Come on, mate. Hit it.'

Pa did a combination:

Flump. Flump. Flump.

'You piss me about, Dom, we start the clock again!'

He didn't have to be so rude about it.

'Get your feet in distance!'

Pa shuffled his feet. Otis jabbed his finger. The patio lights pinged on, sent his jagged shadow streaking across the patio.

Flump.

'Pathetic, Dom. Come on, mate, hit it!'

Flump. Flump.

'Hit the fucking bag!'

Otis always rucked us. Ruckin, that's what we boxers call it. Did I tell you Pa caved in, on account of the getting picked on at school, and let Otis teach me boxing? Well, anyway, ruckin's part of the training. You have to get used to it. Not like this, though.

Tap-tap. Tap-tap. Pa had done all right by his standards. I didn't get it.

Flump. Flump. Flump.

Otis grabbed him by the shoulders spun him round, got his face in close and hissed,

'I Want To See Your Anger, Dominic.'

Spit landed on Pa's face. Otis spun Pa back and shoved him at the bag. Pa tapped his glove against his nose to get the sweat off, breathed out hard, eyes burning.

'Do it, mate.'

Yeah, do it. Put one – *Bam!* – on Otis's bossy mouth.

Tap-tap.

I could do twenty on one foot and twenty on the other. In case you don't know anything about skipping, that's really brilliant.

Pa did it, really did it. Pounded the bag, pounded it, grunted deep as each hard punch went in.

Terrible punches, all power, no technique.

Otis didn't mind.

'Not at the man. Through the man,' he said, like Pa was hitting someone real.

Streetlights crackled and came on.

Otis said, 'Time up,' but quietly.

Pa wouldn't have heard him if he'd screamed it in his face. Pa was in another place, punching harder, harder, harder, punching on and on and on.

I reached one hundred skips and moved on to my stretching exercises.

Pa thrashed and thrashed the bag til he was all thrashed out, then slumped on it, arms wrapped round it, weeping.

Pa wept.

Otis moved towards him, hugged Pa and the bag together, hummed, 'Let it out, let it go, let it out, mate.' Pa gulped and sobbed into Otis's huge chest.

Through his tears Pa whispered something I couldn't hear on account of the tube train rumbling by. Lights disappeared into the night, then I heard him.

'It's the not knowing. The not knowing. The not knowing.' That's what he was saying.

I looked again at Pa's thin hair, his bony shoulders, the flatness where his bum used to be, his skinny legs. It wasn't Aids. It wasn't cancer. It was the not knowing that was eating Pa away. I wound my rope up, did it neatly, the special way, how Otis liked it.

28

Pa slammed the car boot harder than he needed to. Mo hugged that crinkly leather bag she carried everywhere, it used to be her mum's, held it close like any minute a man might snatch it off her. Pa held her door open. She wouldn't get in. She turned, instead, and screamed, there in our street,

'We Can't Leave Harry!'

Air whooshed out of me like I'd taken one of those upper cuts to the solar plexus Otis taught me.

'I'll be fine, Mo. Honest, Mo.'

'Harry! Are You Sure?'

Was I sure? Ten days in rainy Scotland with Mad Mo and Shrinking Pa. Or ten days with Joan and Otis, a fit black real-life fire-fighter picking me up from school every day. Was I sure?

'Mo, we'll look after him.' said Joan. 'Otis'll kill me if I let Harry go.'

We all tensed up.

Otis'll kill me.

You don't realise people talk like that until your little brother disappears.

*   *   *

Once, I started an experiment, planned to make a bar-chart, maybe discover the violentest day of the week.

Day one, 7.15am:

'Point that at me and you're fuckin dead meat.'

A little girl said that down in the square. I wrote it in one of the notebooks Mo gave me when she chucked her work things out.

Assembly:

'I'll fuckin kill ya.'

One of the infants to Parimal. I don't know what Parimal had done. A few kids felt that way about him.

First lesson:

'I could murder a Mars Bar.'

Piggy.

I wrote it down and drew a line:

'9.25am, experiment cancelled.'

H. Pickles, Scientist.

It was just too depressing.

I glanced at Mo to check the damage. Dark-eyed and angry. Head too big for her body. It was all right. That's how she looked these days.

Pa stood behind her, twisting his hands like he was squeezing out the dishcloth.

'Time to go.'

'Harry! Are You Sure?'

Joan pressed a hand on my shoulder, took it away sharpish.

'You and Dom have got some serious work to do, Mo. It's the best thing for Harry.'

They were going with all their troubles to the Isle of

Mull, because grown-ups believe that being somewhere wet and beautiful can do you good.

Mo squeezed my head in both her hands, kissed me with hard, dry lips, then fell into Joan's arms. Pa threw his arms around me, rammed my nose into his chest and crunched my ribs. They'd best not do any cuddling on this holiday. They didn't know their own strength.

They were all packed up, waved off and rolling away when Shy Geoffrey gangled out of his house, waving some papers. Geoffrey was richer than he looked. He had a whole entire extra house just for the holidays. That's where they were off to.

For one horrid moment I thought he was going to say it had fallen off a cliff or something and they'd have to stay at home. But it was all right, he'd only found an extra map. He leaned into Pa's window, mumbling about routes. I could almost hear Pa asking politely if he had any break-ables and would he mind if some of them were acciden-tally broken.

Geoffrey scooted inside. Mo stuck her head out the window, a pinched, panicky look on her face. Pa made one sad *toot* on the horn, and they were off.

I did what I hoped was the right sort of wave.

In my mind they were in Scotland already, screeching round hairpin bends. Pa, squeezing the wheel, snaps,

'How could you, Mo?'

She screams, 'I'm thirty-nine!'

He turns towards her.

'Say that again and I'll –'

The Volvo slides off the road, mows down trees, flips up and rolls. Rolls, rolls, down the ravine. At the bottom it stops.

Silence.

Then,

Bang! Bedang! Bang!

My whole class comes to the funeral. Miss Bliss has never seen a boy so brave. At the reception there's Tizer and Mars Bars, all the sweets that come in black. I make a fantastic orphan, the only one in our school. My boy rating soars. Joan has babies. Three, maybe four. We get a dog and a television.

Back in the house, Joan said, 'You've perked up a bit.'

Otis took me to Basecuts on the Portobello Road and told a man with a four-centimetre nail through his eyebrow to do whatever he wanted, 'but nothing too radical, all right, mate?'

'I Paulo,' said the man.

He was completely bald and wore his trousers open at the top. Calvin Kleins showing. His T-shirt was so thin I saw his, you know, nipples. He ran his fingers through my hair and reached a knot.

He said, 'Iz Problem,' clicked his fingers at the thin girl sweeping up, and walked off.

I looked at Otis. He wheeled his chair in closer.

'The thing is, Harry, trust the professionals. If Paulo's house was on fire I wouldn't want him telling me how to put it out. So I'm not gonna tell him how to cut my hair, now, am I?'

'But it's not your hair, Otis.' He wasn't having a haircut.

* * *

Paulo did a good job, actually. I could see from my reflection in Starbucks.

'We need to get you kitted out, mate. Call it an early birthday present. Can I be honest with you?'

'My birthday's not for weeks.'

'Your clothes, mate, they're a disaster.'

In Starbucks window, a skinny boy, sad face on him, faded tracksuit bottoms squeezing his nuts, way sad trainers pinching his toes. Woolly school jumper, Barbados T-shirt he wore every day. If bag ladies had kids they'd look like this.

'I'm gonna tell you about clothes, Harry.'

We took high stools looking out on the street. Otis set down two café lattes, extra chocolate for me, no cinnamon, lots of froth.

'You don't say, I'm gonna dress like Otis or I'm gonna dress like David Beckham or, God forbid, I'm gonna dress like Dominic. The trick is, look around you, see what you like, see what suits Harry. The clothes, you see, is an expression of yourself.'

I looked at him, really looked at him, seemed like the first time I really had. The cloth on him was heavy, the black really black. He had on close-fitting trousers, not too tight, with a belt, a buckle on it, not flashy, just strong, cool and, well, Otis. His jersey showed off his muscles, the neck on it dipped down into the small dark pit under his Adam's apple. On top of that he had a long-sleeved tan shirt, hanging open. I touched it. Leathery stuff that's soft and warm.

A dressed-up black woman shimmied past a table on the street. Her head swivelled round and through the window came a look so hot it burned my cheek.

My uncle knew how to dress.

'Now, look,' he said.

People out there must have had clothes on before. I hadn't noticed.

I saw a redheaded woman in a slinky skin-tight blouse and trousers with the waist at her hips, high-heeled boots that seemed to be made out of snakes.

I saw purple flares and furry white jackets.

Market traders in old woolly jumpers, don't-fuck-with-me scars on their faces.

Old ladies in surgical shoes, towing shopping trolleys.

Big-school black boys in baggy trousers, the crotch at their knees.

A baby, stripy hat on it, trailing bobbles and bells.

A white man lying across Ladbrokes doorway, fast asleep, blanket on top of him, his hand reaching out to the beer can he'd spilt, fizzy mess on the pavement. I felt sad and panicky. He was the only one I could point to and whisper,

'Otis. That's how I feel.'

He sipped his coffee, came up with a creamy moustache that cheered me a bit. He patted it with a napkin, checked his reflection in the sugar shaker.

'It may be how you feel right now, but it's not what you are, not how you want to be. Dress how you want to be, man. First thing, start looking, start thinking. You've started already. Good man, Harry. Well done. Today we buy one outfit, keep it simple. You wear it, you like it, you think what might go with it. Sometimes you make a mistake. No worries. You should see the mistakes in my wardrobe.'

He should keep his voice down. I looked around me,

hoped those Japanese tourists sipping espressos couldn't speak English.

I whispered, 'Otis, isn't it a bit, well, you know, gay?'

'You're right in a way, mate. You don't talk to the girls about it. You don't say, me and my mate had a thirty pound haircut, sat in Starbucks drinking café latte, checking out threads. And there's men who don't get it. You only have to look at them. Don't talk about it. Just do it. And women like it. Believe me, the women like it.'

'But, Otis, I'm not even ten.' I didn't want dressed-up women with big bazongers burning red marks on my face.

'And you're gonna be a ten year old who feels happy in his clothes, that's all Harry. It's nuffink to get hung up about. You put the work in, you do the looking, you do the buying, then you put your clothes on and fuhgedabar-did, get on with your life.'

We bought everything, even pants. Soft boxers were the thing to wear, Otis said, close to home, on a quiet bit of the street where no-one was about.

'Just so's you know, Harry, and this is man's talk. I never wear the same boxers or T-shirt two days running. Next to your skin? In the washbin. Shower every morning, every night. Working out? Shower straight after. The kit? In the wash. All of it. Don't want sweaty kit hangin around. Some men think it's macho, but you know what?'

Was Otis normal?

'That's all they got hangin around.'

We reached the square. Otis opened the gate.

'That teacher of yours,' he said softly, 'Miss Paradise?'

I thought of Miss Bliss, how she liked men who cried, of Otis and the secret and the way women looked at him, of Joan, just a minute away, most likely frying plantains for me.

'She's got a moustache, Otis. Creaky knees.'

'What?'

'Why do you want to know?'

'Thought I might ask your Miss Heaven if she'd like to bring the class down the station. Whadya think?'

'Emanuela Balisciano. We call her Miss Bliss. It's a brilliant idea.'

Otis and Joan had decided to give me a serious makeover. They didn't say so, but I knew what they were up to. The best bits were watching videos with Otis – the boxing greats, you know, Ali, Foreman, the Rumble in the Jungle, and going to see Tottenham play live in the actual White Hart Lane stadium. Sol Campbell was brilliant! Scored a blinder! The worst bits were eating fish and doing press-ups, which Otis said Sol Campbell did a lot of.

Otis wanted to see how come I was crap at football. We went down the park for a kick-around.

One, two minutes in, he said,

'You can't kick straight –'

'I know that.'

'Let me finish, Harry. You can't kick straight. When d'you get those boots?'

'Before, you know.'

'Long time before?'

It was hard to remember before.

'Tell me when it hurts.'

He squeezed my toes.

'Jesus, Otis!'

'Less of your blasphemy. You can't kick straight, mate, cos your boots is too small.'

So they got me some new ones and we worked on technique. Seemed Otis and Joan could fix anything.

'Joan, do you think they'll be better?'

It was all I could think about, Mo and Pa jumping out of the car, bursting into the house, weighed down only by presents for me.

She stopped chopping onions, wiped her hands on a dishcloth.

'We shouldn't expect much, H. The thing is, honey, sometimes pain brings people together and sometimes it tears them apart. They've had a little holiday, that's all.'

'But one day they'll get over it.'

She sat down, pulled her chair close. If I'd moved my hand a bit I could have touched her giant belly. She went quiet, like grown-ups do before they tell you something horrid.

Otis, shiny-wet and laughing, burst in, a towel round him. He backed out sharpish, leaving wet footprints and the smell of that coconut stuff he slopped on his hair.

Joan said, 'Harry, they will never get over it.'

His hair went tight and springy when he washed it and it felt completely dry.

'Harry,' Joan said in a slow sad whisper like she didn't want herself to hear. 'This is important, Harry. I said they will never get over it.'

I watched Otis's footprints dry and fade.

'Nor will you and nor will we. We've lost Daniel and we will never ever get over it.'

I felt a dark rainy night, a black motorway, engine noise, the taste of petrol in my mouth. I'd be ancient – I mean, like, forty – stuck in the car, telling it to crash, but it wouldn't crash. It would go on and on.

'It won't always be this hard,' Joan was saying. 'The pain of it will lessen, we'll feel it less often, have more easy days between.'

She took my hands. Hers smelt of onion.

'Eventually this awful pain will become, I don't know, something that's there, that isn't our fault, we didn't do something wrong, Harry. But it never goes away. It's always there, part of our landscape. It's part of your landscape, Harry.'

She seemed to be offering me some kind of rescue that did not involve drowning. I didn't understand it, not all of it, not then.

'But, Joan, we can't just, I mean, we've got to –'

'Do something?'

'Yes! Yes!'

'Harry, we're doing it, now. We're just starting, we're just beginning to –'

'To what?'

'Harry, love, we're learning to grieve. That's your mission, our mission, all of us, now, we have to learn how to grieve.'

I checked Otis's footprints. The balls of his feet were all that was left. I could still smell the coconut, though.

'Joan, do you still cry about Daniel?'

'Every day, H. Every day.'

As if to prove it, tears started on the rims of her eyes, fattened up and spilled down her face.

'You don't think he's coming back, do you, Auntie Joan?'

'I don't think he is,' she said.

We sat there til Otis's footprints had completely disappeared.

I whispered, 'Joan, I see Daniel.'

'What, Harry?'

'I see Daniel. I mean, not him exactly. Boys, girls too, just like him. Everywhere. Grown-ups, sometimes. Then, I look again and see they're not like him at all.'

For all I didn't want to frighten her, I'd got going now and found I couldn't stop.

'Things, as well, Joan. Things, like yesterday I saw him hiding by the wall next to the church but it wasn't him. It wasn't. Joan . . .' I choked back tears. 'It was the bin bags.'

'Yes,' she said, as if I hadn't just owned up to her that I was mad as Mo. 'It happens, love. That's how it is. We're looking for Daniel. In our hearts, Harry, we'll always be looking for Daniel.'

'You see him too?'

'Of course, love. Mo and Dom and Otis too. All of us. Everyone. All over the world, in fact. It happens to everyone who's lost someone they love.'

Really, truly? In Italy, Japan and Pakistan and Wakkatoo, all over the world, boys, like me, looking for the Daniel they'd lost? Seeing him, not seeing him at all?

It helped a bit, made me feel not so alone. Like backing Spurs. Or eating fish same time as Sol, most likely. Or being a boxer, me, Otis, Pa and Muhammad Ali.

Joan wiped my tears off with her oniony thumb, then

light flashed out of her, she yanked my hand and pulled her jumper up.

'Feel this,' she said, and pressed my hand into her belly. 'Feel this, the baby's moving.'

So?

I felt . . . nothing.

'Press harder. You can't hurt it. Relax your hand and press harder.'

If it mattered so much to her I'd go along with it. As long as it didn't mean touching her titties.

Nothing happened. Not a thing. And then a feeling, quick and shy but real, like the twitch of my line when the mackerel takes the hook. Made me laugh. Laugh out loud.

'That's your cousin,' she said, and I knew it was true.

Me, Mo and Pa

29

'Do you talk about me?'

'Course we do, darling.'

'What about me?'

I was lying on Mo and Pa's bed, on my back, propped up on the pillows, my hands linked behind my head, my legs dangling off the side. I watched her making up at the mirror. It was worth watching again. She took time and care.

'What about me, Mo?'

She'd had a haircut. It looked quite nice. Not so shiny any more, and there was grey in it, thick stringy hairs. I could maybe offer to pull them out for her. Maybe not.

'I don't know,' she said, 'good things.' She speared her ear, wrinkled her nose. I wrinkled mine. She stuck it all the way through.

'What, exactly?'

I wanted Mo and Pa to tell the counsellor the stuff they used to tell me, you know, that I was brilliant, fantastic, made them glad to be alive. That kind of thing. They'd been seeing her for a whole entire hour every week since they came back from Scotland, no breaks for tea and biscuits, yap yap yap for an hour. I'd lost count of the weeks. Half term had come and gone. Hours, hours and hours. Thousands and thousands of minutes. How could they fill all those millions of seconds without saying loads about me?

'We talk about how you've been affected.' That's all she came up with.

She had an eyelash on her cheek. She leaned into the mirror, flicked it off. Her silver-speckled eyebrows snuggled closer together. I could see right down her bazongers. They were flatter than before. Wrinkly, too.

'And?'

'What, darling?' She smiled at me through the mirror, pulled out her mascara brush – *plop* – and brushed it on. Strong, quick strokes.

'And what else, Mo? I mean, is that all?'

Mascara always made me nervous. You'd think that if you did it every day, the odds on poking out your eye would be quite high.

She got her chin up, did the top deck, blacked the lashes, didn't get that muck all down her face.

'It's a big subject, darling.'

Funny how you could forget how to speak, how to write, how to walk, how to cuddle, how to think, how to sleep, how to cook, how to eat, how to dress, how to drive, forget, forget, forget you had a son, but you could still get your mascara on clean.

'How do you know?' I heard my voice, cold, cold. I swung my legs, kicked my heels hard against the bed base.

'I know a bit about you, Harry.'

'How do you know how I'm affected?'

'I do live with you, darling,' she said softly. 'I am your mother.'

She seemed to be backing away. She wasn't. I mean, really, she was sat right there in front of me, trapped, but in her face I could see that she was backing away.

'You never ask me, Mo.'

She turned around to face me. One eye was all made up. The other wasn't. It made her shock seem bigger, made her look easy to hurt.

I was only saying. It was only words. They didn't seem so dangerous when I was talking to the mirror.

'I'm asking you now.' Her voice was soft and thin. I wanted to stop anything hurting her.

Too late. I was rolling.

'You're not, you're not asking, not really, no, you're not.'

'I am, I want to know. Harry, please, darling.' She swallowed tears.

'You don't. You're only asking now because I mentioned it.'

'Darling, I'm sorry I never asked before. I can't believe I . . . But if you say so I believe you. And I'm sorry. I'm so, so sorry. I really am. Harry, darling, I'm listening now. Talk to me.'

I didn't know the answer, I had forgotten the question. I didn't know the point of the stupid conversation. Wished I hadn't started it. I only wanted to serve her right for going out of her mind over Daniel and not being glad she had me.

She sat there, one eye done to face the world and the square and the walk down Lancaster Road and the cab ride and the counsellor, one eye the real Mo, the wounded Mo, trying to be brave, like this was part of her punishment and she was going to take it.

In the mirror I saw me, lying like a wanker on the bed, kicking my heels against the wood because I knew she didn't like it. I had to stop it, get me out of there.

'You wouldn't understand,' I said, I don't know why, I didn't mean it, maybe because it was one way to hurt your mum, maybe just to get me out of there.

I stomped off to my bed. Before my tagliatelle. Before the sitter came. Didn't brush my teeth. Didn't pee. So what if Mo got wet sheets and dog's breath in the morning? Pulled off my clothes. Threw them on the floor. Trod on them. Sat on the bed. Hoped I had a stinky bumhole. Didn't like to check in case it was. Stuck a finger up my nose. Found a big dry bogey. Picked at it. Came away with a tug and a salty wet tail. Licked it. Wiped my finger on the sheet under my pillow. Each bad stupid childish thing I did made me feel worse.

I lay awake in the half-light feeling hungry, mean and stupid.

'Sebastiano!' called his mum. 'Five minutes!'

I wished it was me out there in the bushes. I could live on nuts and berries, Walkers Crisps. I wouldn't have to talk to anyone and no-one would get hurt. I could climb out my window, shin down the drainpipe, now, and set up camp.

D'dee D'dee said a train. *D'dee D'dee.*

I saw myself running from the bushes, my boxer's legs powering me out of the square and along Barlby Road, a superhuman leap up, up, up onto the bridge, onto the track, racing, sprinting through the noisy, rattling night after the train, jumping on and clambering on top. Gripping on and riding over Latimer Road and Shepherd's Bush and Goldhawk Road, far, far, far away, away from this, away from here, off to another place completely.

Then I remembered it was the pinky line that only went as far as Hammersmith.

30

Pa said, 'It doesn't mean we've given up.'

'We're just acknowledging our loss,' said Mo. 'So far, what we've lost.'

The grey-black sky leaned heavy on our heads. Black oil, the river looked like, sucked us down. Those coal-black trains thundering behind might pitch us over. Seemed like magic we three stayed standing on the bridge.

Pa held Dan's book bag. Inside, the special stuff we had to throw into the river, and a brick.

We'd had all kinds of things laid out on Daniel's bed.

'Please, Dom. Not those.'

Mo held his Superman jimjams to her face and breathed him in.

Pa touched the birthday scarf Dan knitted. Not a scarf, an egg cosy in fact, on account of how he ran out of time.

'It's only symbolic,' Pa said. 'We don't have to part with anything we don't want to.'

I took back his Jurassic Park pencil case.

*   *   *

'Shall we?' said Pa.

Mo swallowed. 'Let me.'

Pa said, 'We don't want it falling short, hun.'

Below us, on a rusty barge, a man in a donkey jacket hauled rope.

Pa passed her the bag, but held on.

I thought of Otis and Joan and To Have And To Hold.

'You sure, Mo?'

'Do you doubt me, Dom?' she said in that half-laughing voice I hadn't heard since, before.

Pa let go of the bag, gripped her with his eyes, said like he really meant it,

'I don't doubt you, Mo.'

It wasn't her throwing arm he was talking about.

I squeezed between them, closed my eyes to keep the tears in, felt Pa on one side, clench, Mo, breathe in, stretch back, let loose a cry and a throw.

We had to wait for the

plop.

Into the deep, with the brick, went the photo Pa showed people the night we lost him, some hair Mo saved from his David Beckham buzz-cut. And one potato, Lurpak mashed in, wrapped in tin-foil, still warm – I baked it myself.

31

After all that crazy stuff with Terry, I felt a bit nervous of knives. I said, nice and casual,

'What you got there, Mo?'

'Ah, now,' she said, slipping our best cook's knife into her mum's leather bag. 'Alastair has the grinder in today.'

'You what?'

'The word is sorry, darling. I said Alastair has the grinder, the knife grinder in today. He said if we should need anything sharpening to drop it by at the restaurant.'

'Can't he just lend us the grinder?'

'It's a person, darling. You must have seen him. Blind man. Sits at that bicycle contraption outside the restaurant, grinding knives.' She gave me a quick zip of a smile as she zipped up her bag.

A blind grinder on a bicycle contraption? Obviously she was going off again.

I said, 'Do we have to do it now?' We were off up Portobello market to buy our food.

She said, 'We do indeed. He's leaving at noon and it's nearly noon now.'

I looked up at the clock with no tocks. She had the time right anyway.

Out in the square Cal and the big guys, Jamal and Hairy Zac, were doing their thing to Cal's brand new, like portable DJ equipment, I don't know what you call it, but it's brilliant. They didn't say hello on account of they were busy being hard, with their shirts off and drying-up cloths round their heads and baggy trousers hanging off them, key-ring chains down to their knees, but they did stop belting out the words, you know, the seriously dirty ones, and only mouthed them until after we'd gone by.

'My God!' Mo said. She knew the f-word, said it now and then, but she'd most likely never heard it with a 'mother' at the front. It must have shocked her.

Actually, it wasn't that.

'My God!' she said. 'The blossoms are here already,' and she looked about her at all the trees sprouting fluffy pinks and whites I hadn't even noticed.

I said, 'Nice, innit?'

She said, 'Not innit, izz-unt-it,' and then she said like she was talking in a dream, 'Mmmm. Nice energy. Tupac, is it?'

'What?'

'Tupac Shakur. You haven't heard of him?' That's what she actually said. The thing about Mo is, even after, she could still surprise you.

He wasn't there, of course. I didn't think he would be. Just that nice Italian waiter in his bright white apron sweeping the street around the tables, and the usual smelly drunk who hung around most days threatening to ruin it for all

the posh people until the nice Italian waiter gave him half
a pack of fags to bugger off.

The waiter nodded. 'Looks like thunder.'

It was one of those warm, still, muggy days that aches
your head and fills the air with tiny black flies and the *boom
boom judda judda* of people's sound systems they have in their
cars.

Mo nodded back, not the way she used to, my Mo, happy
Mo, but the new way that said, 'Can't you see I have pain?
Look away.'

'He's not here,' I said.

'Ah, well,' she said with a zippy smile and kept on walking past the second-hand clothes shop that smelled of
Granma and the pub that had sick on the pavement, fresh
every morning, seemed like, same place, fresh sick.

I had thought she was coming on. You know, she could
shop again. It doesn't sound like a top marks achievement,
but when you've been completely bonkers buying grapes,
tomatoes, bread and all that stuff can be quite difficult,
especially on Portobello. You have to watch out for your
feet and for your pockets and for a hundred stupid tourists
who stop and ask you where's the market and you have
to tell them that they're in it. But she could do it. Not
like before when she really had, you know, that sort of
happy power that made crowds part for her, that got those
scar-faced market men sharing the craic, that made the
mean old Spanish oil woman with her grizzly mouth
throw in an extra spoon of pesto, free. I don't know what
you call it but Mo didn't have it any more. It was gone,
like snatched by aliens, and they'd left her with that creaky
something in her walk, the way she held her shoulders,

257

clenched her jaw. But she could shop again. She could go out with an empty rucksack and bring it back half full. And that's good, isn't it?

I saw the woman first. We'd almost done our shopping when I saw her. She said, 'Mo,' and left her mouth half open like she didn't know what to do with it.

I patted Mo.

'Ah,' she said when finally she'd got herself focussed. 'Ah, good morning to you, Brenda. It's been a while.'

Brenda was covered in freckles, had a floppy tie-dye T-shirt and a Body Shop cloth bag with celery sticking out. Brenda looked exactly the sort of person who'd send those stupid silver balls.

'Mo, it's you.' She was a turkey lady, no chin where it's supposed to be and then a jangly load of fat all down her neck. It jangled now.

'Indeed,' said Mo.

I wanted Mo to move, keep moving, but we were at the narrow bit where Elephant's Antiques spilled out onto the pavement and nudged into the grapefruit man and the Brenda Beazley person had got the space wedged tight with her old lady's shopping trolley and seemed busy fiddling with something just behind her, a dog or something, hiding it behind her back.

'I, I,' said Brenda Beazley.

People clucked and cursed and backed away and walked, still tutting, cussing, right around the grapefruit man. Dark clouds moved, I felt a chill, smelt the rain that would be coming.

'I, I. We. I mean, my partner too . . .'

I checked to see if we could go back the way we'd come but there were people pressed behind us. I tried to figure out a way past her, but Brenda bloody Beazley had got the whole street jammed. That's when I saw the thing that she was hiding. A boy. The Beazley boy. She'd got him pushed behind one of those battered wardrobes that Mr Elephant said came from Ancient Sinatra or some other place you've never heard of and Cal's dad said came from a garage under the motorway where men with leather belts whacked ten kinds of shit out of it to make it look old. That's what she was hiding, the boy who'd got born same day as Daniel. He looked a bit like Daniel, but kind of thick and not much fun. I looked at Mo. She'd seen him too. I looked at Mo and I remembered the knife.

'All of us,' said Brenda Beazley, 'It's too, too . . .'

That boy stuck out his freckly face from back behind the wardrobe.

'Behind you!' I wanted to shout, like when Mr Pratt was Cinderella. 'He's behind you!'

'We. Of all people. Feeeeel,' she said like she felt things more than anyone. Next thing she felt was a sharp tug on her tie-dye T-shirt. Her son. She pushed her bag in front of him, shoved her celery hard against his face.

I saw Mo unzip her bag and make the zippy smile, the boy peek out, Brenda freeze and Mo take out the knife and, 'Hello, there,' and Mo pull back her arm and stick the knife, stick the knife . . .

It didn't happen, though.

'So kind.' That's what Mo said, and with the quick tight smile that I remembered from before, the one she'd never

259

use on us, that said, 'I have no time for you.'

'It was nothing,' said Brenda Beazley. 'But. What can you? What can one? What is there to —'

'Nothing,' said Mo. 'There's nothing to say. Cheerio!'

She held out her hand and I took it. It's not as if my mates could see. Together we moved forward. Brenda Beazley backed behind the wardrobe with her boy and as we passed Mo let go my hand and put her arm around my shoulder, wheeled us round and said like she was introducing the undisputed heavyweight champion of the world,

'Brenda, this is Harry. My First Son.'

The sky was grey and grumbling, the air had cooled, rain whipped Portobello, and that acne-faced, bloody-aproned man was chopping up our three organic chickens when I saw how Mo had sagged, how much the Beazley boy had cost her. I squeezed her hand. She squeezed mine back.

I said, 'He was big, wasn't he?'

'Yes, my love,' said Mo. 'You forget how fast they grow.'

32

Piggy was called Piggy because he squealed like a pig. Really, exactly like a pig. That's how I knew when I rounded the school gates and heard a pig squealing that it was Piggy in trouble.

I ran across the road into the estate, to the bearpit, the tiny playground we weren't supposed to go in on account of fights and squishy condoms and needles and crisp packets smeared with glue.

I ran to join Terry, Peter and the guys leaned against the wall, and looked down.

Bam! Bam! Bam!
    What? How'd Piggy get into this?
    Piggy taking punches like a big fat punch-bag.
Bam! Bam!
    His idea of fighting is sitting on you til you shout, 'Submit!' Fighting for laughs.
Bam! Bam!
    This isn't fair.
    Terry's shouting, 'Fight, Piggy. Fight, man.'
    Like Piggy has a chance.

This isn't right.

There's a big guy hitting him, a posh school kid in those stupid yellow britches. Not gay like the rest of them. Big. Fighter's legs on him. Nice footwork. Hard punch.

Bam! he goes. *Bam!*

Posh Boy feints a punch. Piggy cringes, wobbles, squeals.

Terry's screaming, 'Take him, Piggy! Be a man!'

Peter's sweating. Muscle in his jaw is twitching. Pete grabs Terry's arm.

'You've got to stop this, Tel. He's getting hurt.'

'You're not turning chicken on me, are you?'

Small dark stain in Piggy's trousers, getting bigger.

'What's the matter, Piggy?' Posh Boy sneers. 'Need the lavatory?'

No. No. No.

I'm down the steps and in the pit and shoving Posh Boy off. Piggy staggers for the steps. Posh Boy's back on guard in just a second.

'You want it?'

He shows me fists, big hard fists, grazed on Piggy's face.

I don't want it. I just wanted Piggy out of it.

Terry's screaming, 'Kill him, Pickles! Kill him!'

'Breathe,' says Biffo from my corner. 'You're the boss, now breathe and dance and keep him moving.'

I breathe. I dance. Posh Boy's plodding after me.

'Guard up,' says Biffo. 'Keep your guard up.'

The swings go by for, I don't know, the hundredth time. I haven't hit him yet and feels like we've been fighting all our lives.

I move my shoulder, draw my fist back.

Oh. No gloves . . . I'll hurt my hand.

I pull my punch.

Posh Boy tries to pop one in.

I see it coming, yank my chin back, brush the punch off with my arm.

'See that? Kid's all open when he strikes.'

The lads scream, 'Whack im! Punch im! Kick im in the nuts!'

I'm dancing. The balls of my feet are steel springs. It's easy when you're king of the skipping rope.

I've got moves in my head. Feint again. Posh Boy moves in. All open. *Bam* into his ribs. *Bam. Bam. Bam.* Watch him fall.

I feint.

Posh boy moves in.

I –

Boff!

Boingggggggg, I go.

Body jars. Head's tingling, buzzing. Eyes wide open. Suck in air like magic glue. Weheyy! I'm flying! What happened? Was I hit?

'Guard up,' says Biffo. 'Hold off. Dance. Recover.'

No way, Jose. I'm thinking Ali. Rumble in the Jungle. I can take it.

I'm in close, taking punches. I'll let him waste himself.

Jesus, that hurts.

I hold off. Dance. Recover.

'One good punch,' says Biffo. 'All we need.'

Yeah. Upper cut. Under his guard. Up into his solar plexus.

Here's how.

Dance.

Move in flat-footed.

Dig your toes into the ground.

Drive the power, all of it, into the punch.

'Now you're talkin, Kiddo. In through the belly. Up through the lungs.'

Posh Boy throws a loose and lazy roundhouse.

I dodge it, move in. Dig in. Drive the power.

Fast. Up. Hard.

Doooff, it goes.

Not at the boy. Through the boy.

Whoosh!

That's good.

Air goes out of him. He slides down my leg.

I pull back, teeth grinding.

His mouth, stretched tight – puke down his chin. Hand grips his chest.

'Knee him in the face!' Terry screams.

I pull back. The crowd roars. I see Posh Boy in the spotlight. He's going down, down, knees onto the canvas. Only it isn't canvas.

Crack! He's on the concrete, slumped, sobbing, wheezing.

Terry screams, 'Kick him, Pickles!'

I won't. Not because I'm a nice boy. I'm not a boy at all. I'm Ali. He's Sonny Liston. A great big ugly bastard and he's down and out and finished.

I'm standing over him, right fist cocked. Ali.

He looks up, blinks three times. His eyes are wet.

Ali would say something. Finish him that way.

There's no hurry. He's not getting up.

'You're only winded, ya big puff.'

The lads jeer. They like it.

'Ambulanth,' croaks Posh Boy. 'Get an ambulanth.'

Wanker! Thinks he's near dead when he's only been winded.

I say, 'Pith off, ya big wuth. Pith off.'

Silence.

Then they get it and they're laughing, even Piggy, he's grinning all over his fat tear-stained face.

I'm laughing. I'm lippy. I'm king of the world.

'Two hits in it,' murmurs Biffo. 'Kid hits the boy. Boy hits the deck. Fuckin A. Don't need me no more. Kid? You're back in the game.'

Me, Peter and Piggy headed back towards the square. I didn't ask them. They tagged along like in the old days.

Pete said, 'Fuckinell, Harry —'

That was pretty wild for Peter. He never swore. I mean, if you knew him you'd understand that he was all wound up.

'Fuckinell, Harry, where'd you learn to fight like that?'

'Oh, you know. My Uncle Otis showed me some moves.'

Piggy said, 'Glad he did is all I can say, Picks. I think you saved my life.'

I said, 'How'd you get into it, Piggy?'

He blushed at the pavement. 'Nother one of Terry's brilliant schemes.'

Pete said, 'I told you, keep your distance.'

'Yeah, well,' said Piggy. 'Easier said than done.'

I said, 'How come Terry didn't do his SAS karate on the posh kid?'

They both looked kind of shifty.

Piggy said, 'You know what Terry's dad does, Harry?'

'Course. He's SAS.'

'Picks, he's an accountant.'

'That's just a cover story.'

Pete said, 'He really is an accountant, Harry.'

'Days off, though, he's SAS.'

'Picks, days off his dad plays golf.'

'He's full of shit,' said Peter.

'You're hurting me.'

'It's only arnica,' said Pa.

'Imagine he's your patient,' said Mo in her half-laughing way. 'Then you might be a little more . . .'

'Jesus, Pa!'

'. . . gentle.'

'Run me through it one more time,' said Pa, lifting my shirt with one hand, squeezing my ribs with the other.

'Ouch! I fell, all right? It's no big deal, I fell is all.'

I fixed my eyes on the dark yellow oblong where the Picasso used to be.

'Fell onto someone's fist?' he said quietly.

I watched the clock with no tocks.

'Hey, Pa, you'd better shift it. You'll be late for surgery.'

He let go my shirt. 'Nothing broken. You'll . . .'

Live, he was going to say.

'You're right, Harry. I should run.'

I was just thinking I'd got away with it when he took hold of my hands, held the knuckles to the light and leaned back so Mo could have a good gawp too.

'I see the other fellow took a few,' she said.

'Too right. You should have seen him,' I blurted, like a moron.

They cleared the dinner things. I lay in bed and wondered about all that stuff they never told me until the counsellor told them to.

About how army cadets and police on their knees had searched whole entire fields with their fingertips.

About the helicopters, sniffer dogs, police frogmen too.

About sightings in Bradford and Glasgow, Pontefract, Brighton and a few other places.

About the stupid creepy man who went to prison for saying he knew all about Daniel when he didn't know zip.

About how Mo and Pa went on the telly to beg for Dan back.

Seemed the whole country had been out looking for Daniel. They should have told me before. It might have saved a lot of trouble. I suppose we just stopped talking for a while.

D'dee D'dee, said the train. Maybe one of those with office people in crumpled suits who sleep and let their mouths hang open. Some of them been for a drink, now and then burp. *D'dee D'dee.*

To keep from dreaming I listened for the next train, the next one, the one after that.

D'dee D'dee. D'dee D'dee.

They climbed the stairs. Opened my door. Had a good long look at me. *D'dee D'dee. D'dee D'dee.*

They whispered something mushy in the dark.

'Se-bas-ti-ano,' screamed his mum. 'This is the very last time.'

The toilet flushed. Once for him. Once for her. Why not flush it all together? Humungous poos, most likely. Didn't hear them brush their teeth. They must have done it, though.

D'dee D'dee. D'dee D'dee.

I heard Mo howl into her pillow, I heard Pa's soothing mumble. It was all right. It happened every night, most mornings too. We'd got a beat back in our life and that was part of it.

We flew down the fast lane in Joan's crappy Nissan. The driver had one hand on the wheel, wound down the window with the other, clamped something sticky on the roof. Playing cards flew. I gripped the dog cage. Wailers sounded. Cars pulled over.

Daniel, eyes closed, slumped against the door. His poor face bruised and grazed and black with blood.

'Mo! Pa!'

'Quit your shouting, Harry. I can hear you. Everything you need's right there.' Calm, calm. Otis was in charge.

We had to lie on our backs to hoist up the trousers, stiff brown dungarees with built-in boots and silver bands that shimmered in the dark. We sat up, pulled the jackets on, our yellow helmets, proper ones, not plastic.

I looked about me.

'Where's the water tank? Hoses?'

'My department, Harry. Not your problem. You make sure your chin strap's good and tight.'

We swerved off the motorway, bumped across a bumpy field, pulled up maybe sixty metres from the farmhouse. The night flashed and wailed with blues and twos. There were stables, barns and tractors. Windows glowed. The air smelled of bonfires. A red halo pulsed above us. Fire trucks rumbled, men set ladders and pulled hoses. Seemed like everything was made of Lego.

Otis opened up the back. We scrambled out.

'Ready?'

I trotted to keep up with him. Every step the heat grew stronger. The air stung my eyes. I felt my nostrils widen, my chest fill with power. I wasn't scared. I was ready. We were with Otis and he would look after us.

'Come on, Dan! Hurry!'

'He's not coming with us.' Otis, striding on.

Daniel stood, toes out, swinging his little red flowery watering can, the one he got from Woolies with his pocket money, like an idiot.

'He's right,' said Dan. 'It's time for you to go.'

I would have argued, but Otis was a dot already, disappearing into the distance. Anyway, I knew what was required of me.

'Sorry, Daniel.'

'What for?'

'Everything.'

'It's OK, Bro.'

We shook on it. Dan smiled. A rock filled my throat. Tears pricked my eyes. I hugged him so he wouldn't see me crying. Helmets clanked together. I turned and ran with all my strength towards the fire.

33

Otis was the star attraction at my adventure birthday in the park, only he wasn't, on account of how he hadn't turned up. Mo and Pa were staying out of it — she wasn't ready yet for public appearances. I had a pretty good idea they'd gone to buy my present. Pa asked, did I have my Tru-Pro-Lok still, so it wasn't in-line skates.

I broke off from the guys to check on Joan. She sat in the grown-ups' pen. She was big, I mean, like, huge, like she was having triplets any second. And all alone. Unless you count the nice Kiwi playworker whacking shuttlecocks who couldn't leave her post, most likely. And that posh woman in giant sunglasses and a stupid big furry coat — the face on her, you'd think she'd eaten poo. The last person you'd be needing if your baby started coming.

Too busy on the mobile to notice me, Joan's voice stretched thin.

'I know. I've been trying you for ages. . . . . . . I see . . .'

Didn't sound like Otis she was talking to. She'd twisted some hair round her finger — its end was going blue.

'Oh, no.' Her eyes shut tight. 'What time was that? . . . . . . Oh . . . . . . I know, I know, I know the score.'

The fur lady was having an important conversation too. By walkie-talkie. 'Rufus, stop pressing the button! Get your finger orf it, now!'

She got her head up, scanned the playground, fixed her eyes on a big boy in a Barbour jacket standing waiting for the Flying Fox. He had a walkie-talkie and he'd got his back turned on two grumpy girls, pretending they weren't with him. They were shoving gravel in their pockets, like for ammo, probably.

The fur lady put her handset down and screeched across the playground, 'Rufus, get your finger orf the button so Mummy can talk to you!'

The Barbour boy touched his ear as if to say he couldn't hear a thing that she was on about, same poo-faced scowl as what his mum and the grumpy girls had got. It's funny how a family can all look different but all look cross in the exact same way.

'Joan, what's up?'

She bit her lip. 'Ah, Harry. He'll be a little longer than I thought.'

I ran to join the guys. He'd best not be up to his old tricks.

Terry goggled at My Sissay climbing the high, high tower to the Fox. The idea was, she zoomed down the wire, we stood like skittles in the sand. Last one to jump out of the way got points. Terry, Pete and Piggy too had flown the wire so it was my go after My's unless I could slide out of it.

'Hey guys. Guess what? Joan's ten days late. If she starts having contraptions I've got to get her to a hospital.'

'Gruesome,' said Terry.

Pete wrote 'Pacheko' in the sand, like he was too mature for skittles. 'Use my watch if you like. It's got a stop-watch facility.'

Terry said, 'So what?'

'We'll need to time the contraptions.'

I said, 'How long they sposed to be?'

Pete said, 'You find out when you time them.'

'I tell you what, guys, I'll cut the cord,' said Terry. 'I've got this secret tool.'

Piggy – in that stripy sweater he looked just like a skittle – Piggy did a mime behind Terry's back, about the other sort of tool. Terry had on his battle fatigues. I have to say, now I was ten, he looked a prick.

Pete said, 'Safer not to cut the cord unless you know exactly what you're doing.'

Terry said, 'How come you know so much about it?'

'I helped deliver Stanley.'

Piggy snorted, 'That explains a lot.'

Pete gave him a look.

My was at the very top. She'd shred her elbows if she belly flopped in that skimpy pink T-shirt she had on. Not to mention her you-know-whats. Soft little hillocks, not mountains like Mo's. I wondered what they felt like, from the outside.

'Look at me!' she yelled as if we weren't all gawking up at her already.

I should have warned her. It's harder than it looks. There's the drop, for starters. The ground's shifting about. You have to step off the platform, reach out, grab the handle, hope you've timed it right, hope your hands aren't too sweaty, then

273

Wheeeee! You think. I'm flying! Then,

Snag! — your weight catches up with you, and if you're not swinging right,

Twang! go your stomach muscles, you lose your grip, the ground rushes up at you and

Splat!

A boy did that. Wrecked his knees and elbows. Was very brave about it, people said. That Kiwi playworker was really kind to me, to him, I mean.

My stepped out and took the handle. I crossed my fingers, held my breath. She swung into the drop, head back, legs swinging forwards, up. My, a perfect V beneath the wire. Faster than Terry or Peter or Piggy, she swept into the landing bay with a

'Yabba-Dabba-Doo!'

We all dived at once.

'Wicked!' Terry gasped.

It was me she landed closest to. She picked herself up, sneezed four times and said,

'Can't wait to go again.' She smelt of sherbet.

'Go for it,' I said. I wondered where I'd smelt that sherbet smell on somebody before.

Piggy said, 'It's the birthday boy's go.'

'Got to check on the contraptions,' I said and I scarpered.

There'd best not be blood spurting everywhere. I had my best kit on, new Nikes, jersey, v-necked like Otis's, the latest stuff he'd got me, and the cargo pants I didn't really want. Boys in Tupac trousers looked like criminals, he said. Sometimes Otis didn't get it. Maybe Joan could cut the cord herself, what with being a nurse, unless she was too busy groaning in agony or something.

I ran over. She was still on the mobile. She can't have been that worried because she'd done her hair. She'd had it up before and now she had it down.

Rufus slouched by his mother, picked his spots. They'd given up on walkie-talkies and were trying normal talking now, instead.

'I'm bored, bored, bored,' said Rufus.

For all the heat, his mother pulled her fur coat round her.

'Well, Rufie, darling, I have to tell you, love, that makes you rather boring, darling.'

'But, Mummy, I'm so bored.'

'Darling, guard the girls. They're never boring.'

'Forty-four,' I said when I found them at the pull-up bar. They'd moved on from the Flying Fox because those Rufus girls had bugged them.

'You what?' said Peter.

'Forty-four contraptions. Probably forty-five by now. Little ones. She isn't groaning yet.'

The guys explained the deal was we'd all chip in for ice-creams. Whoever did most pull-ups got a double scoop.

Piggy was useless, My did eleven, beating Terry and Peter. I'd perfected a method where you rocked your body into the pull-ups so you did hardly any arm work. It was brilliant. It was Otis's method, actually.

'You're fit,' said My.

'You're fit yourself.' For a girl, I nearly said.

I swung off the bar at my all-time world-record, thirteen pull-ups. Which was handy, because if Otis didn't show I was going to look a total wassock.

Me and Peter ran to get the ice-creams. We passed Rufus kicking flowers up by the trees, his mum's voice squawking out:

'Mummy to Rufus, Mummy to Rufus, what's with the girls? Over.'

'What, what you say? Over.'

'Mummy to Rufus. Get your finger orf the button. Over.'

'Can not read you. Over and Out.'

You could see why he didn't want to bother with those girls. They'd launched a suicide mission up the bamboo tower, shoving past the little kids to the top.

Me and Peter headed off out of the playground for the kiosk by the café. Behind the railings, people laughed and read the papers, drank cappuccinos, like this was any other day.

I said, 'Piggy was a laugh about Terry.'

Pete said, 'Look, a queue.'

I said, 'Piggy was funny, eh, Pete?'

He said, 'Terry's all right, long as you don't believe a single word he says.'

I said, 'You thought he was cool for long enough.'

'Yeah, well,' said Pete, pretending he was interested in some chewing gum on the path.

'You were best mates and everything.'

Pete looked up like he was going to make our order, but this huge family ahead of us were all having weird and complicated combinations.

'What's he doing here, then?' Peter said.

'What?'

'Why've you invited him?'

I said, 'Pete, you can't dump a mate just because he's got ishoos.'

Truth is I wanted Terry to see who was gang leader now. Hard to say. Me, Pete or maybe even Piggy. One thing's for sure. It wasn't Terry.

Pete poked the chewing-gum with his toe and said, 'You were pretty strange, you know?'

That lady with congenital dislocated hip, CHD for short, hobbled by, after her dog. Would I be brave enough one day to cut her open, crunch her hip about and put her right?

Pete said, 'I mean, no reason why you shouldn't be. Strange, I mean. And. Well. Harry. We were younger then.'

I said, 'We're ten now.'

He said, 'Ten's something else.'

I paid for all the ice-creams – I didn't want guys thinking it was the kind of birthday where you had to buy your own. We got all the way back to the playground with no serious spillages and nipped over to give Joan her pistachio. I'd got her two flakes – the extra for the baby. She gave us a smile that didn't involve eyes.

That fur lady paced the grown-up pen like a tiger, which was probably what got killed to make her coat, I bet. She looked happier, puffed on a fag and said,

'Mummy to Rufus, Mummy to Rufus. I think we've got it. Over.'

The play-worker was trying to get her attention but the fur lady just kind of swatted her away.

'Mummy to Rufus, can you hear me? Over.'

'I don't know for sure,' Joan said. 'That's what I'm trying to establish.'

She'd actually pulled some of her hair out.

Screams came from the bamboo tower. The play-worker dropped her badminton racket and ran for it.

'Please check. I know you've had admissions . . . . . . The major incident at Shepherd's Bush . . . . . . Otis. Otis. O for Orange. Otis, as in Redding . . . . . I'm his wife.'

The minute she said major incident I knew why Otis was late. Me and Peter raced to tell the guys.

My tucked into her butterscotch, 'That's only up the road.'

Terry said, 'You can see for miles from the Fox.'

'Too bad it's full,' I said. It really was.

'Let's do the rope wall, then,' said Piggy. 'Eat up, eat up.'

My's bum looked nice in those khakis. I was doing what Otis had taught me. Not looking at girls' bottoms. What he said was,

'Down isn't your business, man. Up and on the level, that's what you is interested in. You have no business, Harry, looking down there.'

My reached the top first, followed by Terry, Peter, Piggy and, last of all, me.

Terry said, 'It doesn't look very major to me.'

He had a point. Blue sky. Fluffy white clouds. No smoke anywhere. I felt Otis's glory slipping away from me.

Pete said, 'How come you know so much about it?'

'My dad was drafted into Kuwait when the oil fields went up.'

'Was he hurt?'

'Injured.'

'Injured where, exactly?'

'In the Gulf.'

'Oh, the Gulf,' said Pete.

My giggled in that silent way she had. I felt it through the rope.

Pete said, 'I tell you what, Terry. I hope your dad doesn't get cancer.' Terry was a bit quiet after that.

Over on the bamboo tower those grumpy girls dropped stones on the play-worker climbing up. Way down in the little kids' playground a boy lay on his back and screamed, thrashed his arms about, kicked his tricycle over. Dan had tantrums that way. I held on and breathed easy like Otis had taught me.

'Maybe we need to be higher,' My said.

'Tip-top, the Fox is free!' Trust Piggy to notice.

We all climbed down.

I said, 'I'll be over in a minute. Just got to check on Joan.'

She'd put her hair back up. It looked a mess.

I said, 'Your hair looks nice.'

She said, 'You've something on your face.'

She licked her thumb to wipe it off. Don't you hate it when they do that? I let her, though. Shame my jersey wasn't the sort that needed tucking in or she could do that for me. I wouldn't mind just then.

'Otis doesn't believe in heroics, does he, Joan?'

She swallowed hard and smiled, 'He's very good at his job.'

She touched her belly.

'Is he kicking?'

'No, babe, sleeping.'

She called Otis babe.

She said, 'What makes you think it's a boy?'

'I just know it, Joan. I'll bet you anything.'

And when he was big enough I'd teach him all the stuff grown-ups don't tell you. Like where the tongues go in kissing and how you keep your own spit in your mouth. Do you ask first or do you go right ahead and do it? I'd tell him all of it. I'd know everything by then.

The Kiwi play-worker had got the fur lady and her girls lined up against another mum and three small, whinging kids.

'We need to think about how our behaviour impacts on others?'

She talked like she was asking questions.

'Francesca, Lolly, you won't be playing here next week?'

Really she was laying down the law.

'And just a polite reminder? This is a no smoking zone?'

'Rufie? Girls? We're orf,' the fur lady snapped as if she had a choice about it. The other mother smiled a quick, mean smile. Rufus grinned.

I tried to remember that joke Joan liked.

Hey Joan! There's a caterpillar in your ice-cream!

Maybe that bit's in the punchline.

I got it:

Joan! Do you like caterpillars?

Yuck! No!

That's a shame, cos you just ate one in your ice-cream!

Only she hadn't ate her ice-cream. It was on the bench, there, melting, the chocolate flakes as well. That's what got me really nervous. She liked her flakes. A wasp wriggled in the goo.

I tried to think of another one, shifted my weight from one foot to the other, put my hands in my pockets, took them out, folded my arms behind my back. I wanted to be with My and the guys, but it was obvious Joan needed me.

That's how come I was the first to see Otis. Not in full kit and helmet like I'd hoped. Just his blue polo shirt with the fireman badge, blue trousers and black shoes. He did have a huge white bandage stuck right across his forehead. He crept up behind Joan, made a little O with his lips, put his finger there to shush me, slipped his hands over her eyes.

She didn't need to say, 'Who's There?'
He didn't need to say, 'Guess Who?'
At his first touch she burst into tears.

He wrapped his arms around her and the bump. Muzzed his face in her hair. A breeze caught up his smell – bonfires, sweat and antiseptic. I breathed it in and turned away.

The trees around the little kids' playground dropped the blossomiest blossom I had ever seen. The colours were so bright they hurt my eyes. That tantrum boy rode his tricycle towards the trees, slowed in a snow of blossom and stopped, hopped off a bit like Daniel did it. He looked straight at me, stuck his tongue out. Served me right for staring. He had a snouty-looking face, not like Dan's at all. Just another little boy.

Pete, My and Piggy called to me from the landing bay. I ran for the Fox, picking up speed. I wanted to tell My and the guys that my uncle was a hero and alive and slightly injured too. I heard happy crowds screaming for the fastest boy runner in the world. I reached the tower and climbed it in long, easy strides. I conquered the summit and took in the view. The crowds didn't know it yet but they were about to witness a world-beating leap. I stepped out, reached up and took hold of the handle. With what breath I had left I yelled,

'Yabba-Dabba-Doo!'

And I flew.

ACKNOWLEDGEMENTS

Sometimes you get lucky. Thank you to everyone who gave more help than I might reasonably ask or expect.

Alex Noble, Hannah Dines and Rachel Dines gave clear-eyed reports from childhood. Liz Rayment-Pickard and the teachers and children of Oxford Gardens Primary School helped me to imagine Harry's school life.

David Remnick's *King of the World* and Norman Mailer's *The Fight* refreshed a guilty passion for boxing. Bill Webster invited me into the Fitzroy Lodge ring and Rod Robertson adjusted the footwork on the page.

Mark Field talked about fire-fighting and heights. Azucena Durán, Cheryl Godkin-Burke and Teresa Mc Sweeney helped with language. Richard McDougall let me believe I could make people laugh.

Hellen Stack advised on child protection. Scott Armstrong gave me the baseball bat, Bill Noble, the clicky hip. Reg Groves let me loose inside his shed.

Janet Malcolmson, of Thames Valley Police, explained police procedure and Peter Jackson gave the words a final frisk.

Esmé Madill was a generous first reader. Useful criticism came from Philip Hensher and Lynne Truss at Arvon's Lumb Bank, and from Philippa Collie-Cousins.

John Murray's critique, paid for by Cumbria County Council, Northern Arts and North West Arts, pushed me to start the whole thing again. PFD's Sarah Ballard did a radical, elegant edit.

Smokey Joe Productions kindly allowed me to quote from Merchant's *Rock It*, by Dennis Williams. Kenny Phillips of KMP did the same for Preacher's *Jump & Wave*, by Barnett Henry.

Warmest thanks are due to my agent, the tenacious Alex Elam at PFD, and to the whole kind and ballsy Canongate team.

Finally, thanks to the man who made the tea, paid the rent and said, 'No Pasaran!' Andrew, you can read it now, if you like.

Clare Sambrook
Cumbria, 2004